AND THE BILLIONAIRE

Miss Guided
AND THE BILLIONAIRE

LORIN GRACE

CURRANT
CREEK PRESS

Cover Design © 2019 LJP Creative
Photos © iStock; Olena_Z

Formatting by LJP Creative
Edits by Eschler Editing

Published by Currant Creek Press
North Logan, Utah

First edition: April 2019
ISBN: 978-1-970148-03-9

Uncle Cordell

THANKS FOR THE SONG.

Misadventures in Love

The tradition of the Miscellaneous Crown traces its roots to sometime in the late sixties or early seventies. The unofficial club was founded by the residents of Marden Hall Women's Dormitory, Bradford Women's College. A Miscellaneous Crown is awarded to any of our alumnae who demonstrate exceptional qualities in precarious circumstances and who remind us how far a sense of humor can carry us.

They awarded the first Miscellaneous Crown in 1974, when Amy G. put her foot in her mouth and was dubbed the first Miss Stepped. However, Mary S., in her biography "I was Miss Informed" claims to have received the first crown in 1968. Since the mid-eighties, crowns mostly made of poster board and foil have been awarded to many of our alumni for any number of titles. A current list of title holders can be found <u>here</u>.

The unofficial song is attributed to the class of 1976 (Parody of Miss America). Please note, the class of '72 claims the words are theirs written during the 1971 national pageant. A few notable graduates, including Dr. T., claim to have sung a similar version to their Johnny Desmond record on the old record player once located in the south corner of the gathering room, possibly as early as 1959.

There she is, Miscellaneous!
There she is, all that's real.
The dreams of all college girls,
who are more than witty,
May come true in any city,
Where she will become the queen of her destiny!

There she is, Miscellaneous!
There she is, all that's real.

With so many choices
She'll take the world by storm
Because she got her start at Marden's Dorm!
And there she is,

Walking on air she is,
Kindest of the kind she is
Miss All-n-any-of-us!

Currently, Ms. Charlotte Wilson, dorm mom since 1992, has the final vote on all nominations.

S end. Gina glanced at the clock. She'd made the deadline with
fifteen minutes to spare. *One project complete, two to go.* The
phrase had run on repeat since she'd become the creative head
of one of New York City's premier advertising firms four months
ago. For everything she completed there was twice as much to do.

To stretch her legs, Gina left her office and walked around the
floor. Most of the employees nodded and smiled.

"Hey Gina, I'm off for the day." Zoe Wilson-Gooding packed
up her bags at her desk. One of the best interns Scott & Ricks
ever contracted, the firm hired her full-time weeks before she
graduated. Despite her marriage to one of the city's wealthiest
men, Zoe continued to work at least thirty hours a week, and that
with a full social calendar.

"I'm just glad to have you on, especially since we are short
a designer or two." Gina leaned against the cubical wall.

"I thought you hired two people last week."

"Yes, but they can't start until late March."

Zoe slung her purse over her shoulder. "See you in the morning."

Gina completed her rounds of the design department and
returned to her office. Not ready to switch gears from the res-
taurant-logo designs she'd sent her client an hour ago to the

running-shoe account, Gina allowed herself a few minutes to surf social media—more specifically her college-dorm alumni page, MisadventuresInLove.com. She loved reading the wacky stories that earned an alumnus a new crown and title, even if it was for somebody she'd never met. She chuckled at the story of a recent grad dubbed "Miss Oriented," authored by Ms. Charlotte Wilson, dorm mom of Marden Hall forever.

Suddenly the screen flickered and dimmed, an odd haze surrounding it. Gina looked at the dry-erase board on her wall to see the same haze and dimming there, too. She covered her right eye, and the haze and flickering lights remained. She covered her left and saw only blackness. She turned back to the monitor and clicked the *x* to close the social media site. Her project planner should be showing on the screen, but instead of words, Gina saw only squiggles.

Deep breaths, deep breaths. Don't panic.

Perhaps it was just a bit of mascara on her contact. Gina pulled solution, a case, and a spare pair of glasses out of her top drawer. Ducking behind her monitor, she pulled out her contacts, knowing some of her coworkers found the process unbearable to watch. The switch to glasses came with robotic precision, twenty years of experience guiding her hands. The left side of the room was now filled with odd halos and shapes, the right side dark. Her eye doctor had warned her about a couple conditions common to high myopes, people with extreme nearsightedness, but those weren't likely to occur until she was older. Gina attempted to quash the panic building inside. How could she work if she was blind?

Her doctor had warned her it might happen years from now, possibly in her sixties, not her thirties. How would she support herself? No one had ever heard of a blind graphic designer.

She fumbled with her keys as she opened the locked drawer in her desk, then pulled out her cell phone. Somebody knocked at the door. Gina looked up but couldn't be sure who stood there.

"Can I help you?"

"I need you to look at the furniture project when you have a moment." It was the flat voice of April. Gina looked to the door as she answered so April could read her lips. "Can I look at your layout in the morning? I've had an emergency come up."

"Sure, I'll calendar a sit-down for your first open spot. Do you need me to do anything?"

"I think I need to leave. Just make sure everybody else doesn't cut out early."

April laughed. "Easier said than done, but I'll stay until I'm finished tonight."

Gina noted she hadn't promised to stay until the end of the day. "Thanks. Will you shut the door?" A soft click confirmed April had understood.

Using the audio-command feature of her phone, Gina said, "Call Dr. Ellis." She had to repeat her request twice before it picked the correct number.

It took her a moment to get through the computerized answering system and to a receptionist. "Hi, this is Gina Swann. I can't see out of my right eye, and things are fuzzy and wiggle out of my left. It happened suddenly." Her voice shook. She took a deep breath.

The receptionist confirmed Gina's birthdate and put her on hold for a moment. She returned to the call, interrupting the canned, meant-to-be-soothing music. "Dr. Ellis will work you in as soon as you can get to the office." Gina hung up and debated between Uber and the car service. She called the car service. She'd make sure she let accounting know this afternoon's pickup was personal.

Gathering her purse and coat, she tried to remember if there was anything else she needed to take home. Gary, the night watchman, would let her back in the building if necessary. She made her way to the elevator. She'd never noticed how the bold purple stripe down the center of the hallway carpeting served as an exit guide. The interior designer deserved kudos. The driver awaited her at the curb. Gina settled into the leather seat and attempted to relax her shoulders. If only she could watch where they were going.

Delete.

Another message from his father, president of Galli-Batiste International.

If staying in bed today had been an option, André would still be there. Negotiating a contract for Galli-Batiste's North American holdings in Montreal was not the way to mark the third anniversary of Justine's death. Twice he'd asked for the CEO of the other company to repeat himself.

The CEO frowned but continued the discussion, switching to French.

Language was not the problem. André answered the question in French, then reverted to English for the sake of the Americans on the team he'd brought with him. "I believe this will be satisfactory. However, I'll need confirmation from Paris before I sign the contract. Since it's nearly four and well past working hours in France, may we finish in the morning?"

Everyone around the table agreed, and a round of handshakes was completed. André gathered his papers and left the conference room. The three-person team waited at the elevator. Tori had her phone open. "I've made reservations for dinner and a show ..." She looked expectantly at him. Too bad her efficiency came with a healthy crush on the boss. No matter how many times he put her off, she'd try again. Tori performed her job with attention to detail and minimal direction, but the inevitable conversation might compel her to seek other employment.

André held up his hand. "You are welcome to do what you wish." He turned to the corporate lawyers, Mr. and Mrs. Worth. His father thought him crazy for hiring the husband-wife legal team, but even he couldn't argue with their results. "Please send the contract to Paris." *My father wants to approve it*. Unlike his father, whose middle name should be "Micromanager," André ran his division of the company with a laissez-faire approach. He hired good people and expected them to perform accordingly. As the elevator opened to the lobby, his phone vibrated and his father's face filled the screen.

"You go ahead. I'll take this call." André said to the team, then swiped the green icon and searched for a private corner.

"Are you ignoring me?"

"*Père*, negotiations took longer than expected. I will send the contract as soon I can."

"Why didn't you answer my texts and emails?"

André found an empty hallway. "I can hardly negotiate from a position of strength if I am running to my father at every turn."

"I feared you might not be strong today."

"Then you should have granted the three days off I requested."

"So you can blame yourself? Move on. Don't look back. You have waited too long."

André covered his eyes with his hand and took a deep breath. "You will be delighted with the terms of the contract. Is there anything else?"

"Yes, you must come back to Paris."

"So you can set me up with some other European heiress? I will be there for *Grand-mère's centième anniversaire* on the second Monday in April."

"Non. I cannot wait for her hundredth birthday. I need you here sooner."

"As you pointed out last week, you need me in the States, *n'est-ce pas*? I still have business in New York."

"Delegate. I want you in Paris before the end of the month."

The call ended without a farewell.

André put the phone back in his pocket. Reopening the New York office and boutique would take less than three weeks of his time if he turned the project over to his team. He had not returned to Paris in the past six months, not since his last fight with Père. His father's expectations and plans were not his. If only Père could see that his cousin Arabelle was the answer. She enjoyed designing and headlined the last three fashion week shows.

André hailed a cab and returned to the hotel.

His team had changed clothes and now waited in the lobby. Tori sauntered over and laid a hand on his arm. "Sure you don't want to come? It's so awkward being a third wheel."

André removed Tori's hand. "Not tonight. I need to rearrange my calendar so I can return to Paris sooner than planned."

Hope sprung in her eyes. André kicked himself. How many hints had she dropped about going to Paris with him? "I'll be leaving you here to oversee the opening of the New York office. Between the opening and what we accomplished today in Montreal, now is not the ideal time to leave."

Tori's smile faded.

"Our ride is here. See you in the morning, André," Mrs. Worth said as she tucked her hand in her husband's arm and waved.

André took the elevator to his suite and ordered dinner, then scrolled through the photos on his computer. Had Justine's hair been so short? Only a terrible husband would forget so much in three years, even if they had only been married half that. Or maybe forgetting was natural. Or maybe he was just as terrible as others claimed when they blamed him for her death.

Gina held the black plastic paddle over her right eye. "O-F-L-C-2." Most of the wavering colors and halos had faded, allowing her to see the line.

"Please cover your left eye."

She read the same line through a thick gray haze—the one line she'd memorized as an eight-year-old. "I can see the letters, but it is like I am looking through thick smoke."

Dr. Ellis had her put her chin in the chin rest and looked in her eyes. He pushed his rolling chair back and signaled to the assistant to turn up the lights. "Do you have headaches often?"

"Once or twice a month." *Or week.*

"You suffered an ocular migraine, more specifically the rarer, retinal migraine. A percentage of regular headache sufferers develop them, although that isn't the only cause. On the bright side, ocular migraines are painless and fade in an hour or so. However, they can interfere with life. What is your profession? Computer heavy? Eye strain may be another factor."

"I am an art director for a public-relations and advertising firm. I am in front of a computer forty-plus hours a week."

The doctor chuckled. "In New York? My guess is closer to sixty. Cut the screen time to under forty, including phone time, reading on your e-reader, etc. With your myopia, eliminating eye strain is always good."

"Will that help with the migraines?"

"It can't hurt. Truth is, ocular migraines are a medical mystery. Do track them in a notebook or on your phone, if you have another one. You may or may not. Ocular migraines can be stress related. Have there been any major changes in your life?"

"Six months ago I was promoted in my department."

"Ah, one of those double-edged-sword changes. Looks good from one side and bad from the other. Short staffed and you are making up for it?"

Gina shrugged.

"I see—as in I see the stress around your eyes. You've been coming here for over ten years now. My professional advice is to take a vacation as soon as you can, preferably without your cell phone being tied to work. We can revisit this in six months at your regular appointment. Call if you see any floaters or anything much different from what you experienced today. Questions?"

She shook her head. She'd lived with poor vision her entire life—the two-year-old with glasses. Contacts kept life manageable.

Adding ocular migraine to the list of potential issues was minor and, as Dr. Ellis had said, painless.

"Let me know if anything changes—I mean, with your vision. Changes in life can be for the better."

Her vision clearer, Gina walked to the nearest subway station. While she waited, she studied her calendar. Ocular migraine, scary name, scary moment, but in the end no more damage than watching a bad movie or living through a blind date. Or a bad movie on a blind date. She laughed because they lasted about the same amount of time.

Vacation? She had weeks saved up, but who had the time to use them? Perhaps she should make time.

A week later, André's checklist had shrunk to a manageable size. He checked his phone to make sure Tori had not added appointments to his calendar for his New York City trip. She hadn't been happy about staying at the LA office, but his business didn't require an entourage. The Worths would arrive on Monday to look over any rental leases and properties that interested him.

The driver pulled over in front of Gooding Tower. André had corresponded with Nick Gooding for months over the possibility of opening a store in the City. After spending the last two days with the realtors representing the Gooding's holdings, it was time to meet with Nick himself.

The receptionist's coat and purse lay on the counter next to her. She must have only come in long enough on the Saturday morning to take care of a few appointments. "Mr. Batiste?" At his nod, she picked up the phone. "André Batiste is here. Thank you." She gathered her things and sprinted out the door.

Odd behavior, even for an American. The elevator across the hall closed behind her.

"André?" The voice drew André's attention to the hallway. Nick Gooding strode forward, his hand extended. "Nice to meet you."

Clasping the offered hand, André nodded.

"I see Maureen made it out of here." Nick checked his watch. "Eleven thirty. She should be on time for her son's game. I don't have staff here on Saturday, but I hosted a delegation from China for brunch, and between interpreters and catering, I needed someone at the desk."

"So not all of your employees sprint out of the office the second a client comes in?"

"She would have left already, but I needed to take a call I couldn't at the front." Nick shut the glass doors between the reception area and the elevator and dimmed the lights. "Come on back."

André followed Nick to a large office where a seating arrangement filled one side of the room and a more formal desk and chairs the other. Nick indicated they sit on the more comfortable couches and chairs. "So, how are you liking our city?" Nick handed André a bottle of water.

"Well enough to consider getting a pied-à-terre. The City suits me better than LA."

"Glad to hear. Anyone who spends much time in the City is better off with at least a modest apartment. Have you seen any residential real estate or just commercial?"

"Commercial. I must ask—do you have pied-à-terre in Paris?"

"My mother does. An anniversary gift from my father. She graciously allows the family to use it." The infectious smile on Nick's face brought one to André's own. "My wife has never been to Paris. I am taking her there in two weeks."

"You are recently married, oui?"

"We wed the day before Christmas Eve."

"You shall love Paris in the spring. I'll email you a list of my favorite spots not in the tourist guidebooks. I plan to be there the first of April as well. Perhaps we could plan a dinner if it will not interfere with your plans."

"Dinner would delight Zoe." The conversation turned back to which properties André preferred. Nick pointed out the flaws

André had missed in two of them, helping him narrow the location to a final choice.

The men shook on the deal. They would leave the rest up to lawyers.

"You are not the typical American businessman. You talked me out of the locations that would have been most lucrative for you. Why?"

Nick shrugged. "Because they would not have been best for you."

Having conducted business on four continents, André was both surprised and pleased to find Nick's reputation as "Do-Gooding" more than a PR ploy.

Nick pulled out his phone. "If you don't have any plans for the next hour, why don't you come to lunch with me and meet my wife? She is meeting with her boss this morning and promised to finish in time for lunch."

The billionaire's wife worked? André was not sure where to put the idea. "I'll admit I am curious to meet a woman who has never been to Paris."

Nick took a coat from the closet and turned off the lights. "Zoe grew up on a farm in Indiana. Until she met me, she'd never owned a designer dress. She is good for me as she views life so differently. Already we have rearranged policies and procedures in many of our subsidiaries based on her input. Someday I hope to lure her away from her design job and convince her to join my board of directors."

André followed Nick to the elevators. "She still works? She wasn't after your money?"

"Actually, she refused to have anything to do with me because of my wealth. First time we met, she wouldn't even speak to me." Nick laughed. "I've never worked so hard for a date in my life. But it was worth it." The newlywed businessman smiled the secret smile of a man who planned on celebrating a fifty-year wedding anniversary a half century from now.

Love. The word echoed in the empty chambers of André's heart. A word he and Justine often said but never felt.

"I can't finish this." Gina pushed her plate of strawberry crêpes back. "How did you talk me into a meeting here?" Lucinda's restaurant should be marked on all city maps as a dieter's downfall.

Zoe lifted her fork. "Bribery works. I used the excuse of Scott & Ricks hiring enough designers to fill the desks to draw you out of the office for one Saturday. Tell me—since you received the promotion, have you taken any full weekends off?"

Gina stiffened. "I went up to Boston for Christmas."

"And took your laptop and finished the Wabble toy campaign. Doesn't count."

Zoe set her fork down and inched the plate away. "I've thought about taking a vacation. Adrian has been after me to use my vacation days. He keeps telling me the place won't fail if I am gone." The cofounder of Scott & Ricks had walked in during her second migraine Wednesday evening. Gina had kept the facts vague, playing down her discomfort as a normal headache, pretending she saw his face clearly, but the lights bothered her. Admitting she couldn't see wouldn't help her career. Adrian Scott had sent her home after calling the car service himself. She remembered his exact words: *"Burning yourself out stifles creativity. Take some time off. Shayne and I can cover things. I miss the day-to-day hands-on design work. By this time next week, I expect you to turn in a vacation-request form with HR."*

"Good for him. I've told you this for a month. You're not just my boss, you're my friend, I see the strain you've been under. You may try to hide your headaches, but we see them. You have more than the normal one a month a manager is obliged to have. Get away from your computer for a while."

"You guys know I have headaches?" At least they were talking about the regular kind now. The ones that drained her supersized bottle of over the counter pain pills.

"The pain shows in your eyes. And what ever happened with the headache that sent you running from the office a week and a half ago? Still has April freaked out."

The day of the first ocular migraine. "What did April say? Does everyone know?"

"I don't think she is saying anything out loud. I am the only other person in the office who signs, so I learn the juicy secrets. She said you looked funny. Squinty-eyed, like you couldn't see her. The biggest red flag is you left. You never leave before the workday ends."

April found excuses to be in Gina's office two and three times a day. Gina traced a design on the table with the handle of her spoon. "Have you heard of ocular migraines?"

"Are they different than the regular head-splitting kind?"

Gina explained the best she could, excluding her fears that if her vision worsened, she wouldn't be able to work as a designer.

"See, even your body wants you to take a vacation." Zoe handed her plate to the waitress and asked for a to-go box.

Gina did the same. "My eye doctor thinks one would be ben-eficial."

Zoe nodded to Gina's ever-present bullet journal. "Show me your bucket list."

"I can't afford anything on it." Gina opened to a well-worn page. She'd illustrated many of the items. A colorful rendition of the *aurora borealis* occupied one corner. From this angle, her illustration resembled the effect of an ocular migraine.

Zoe pointed at the Eiffel Tower. "Paris. Do Paris in the spring."

"I can't afford it."

"Nick and I are going in two weeks. Come with us. Nick's mom owns an apartment as big as our penthouse."

Gina held up her hands. "No way am I crashing with newly-weds in Paris."

"Fine, get a hotel nearby. We don't need to hang out together all the time. Nick said he would spend a couple of the days on business, so we can go to the Louvre or Musée d'Orsay together or shop on the Champs-Élysées."

Gina studied her bucket list. She had copied the list from book to book for the past four years, never checking a single item off other than seeing the Golden Gate Bridge because she had been in San Francisco on business. "I still don't have enough money to do that right now."

"Yes, you do. I'll pay for your flight and hotel."

"You can't pay for me!"

"Seriously? What else can I do with my final paycheck? We don't need it."

"Last paycheck? You can't be leaving me."

"There are great designers out there who need jobs, and to be honest, I feel guilty working. Now that you hired the new employees, I can leave without worrying about you. Besides, Adrian is letting me keep my desk to work pro-bono jobs."

"Of course he is. Most of those jobs are for Gooding Charities, and since the Goodings own the building ..."

"Yet another reason to quit. It is difficult to work for a company your husband partially owns."

"Don't you own it too?"

"Probably. I try not to think about that. So weird." Zoe shuddered. "But the point is, I don't need my paycheck. You helped me out so much last fall. Let me do this. A plane ticket and hotel. I'll even use one of the budget sites—with two caveats. I get you on our plane and the hotel is in walking distance of the apartment."

Gina bit her lip. Paris was within reach.

"If you turn me down, I'll just do something stupid like buy an overpriced pair of shoes. I don't own Jimmy Choos yet." Turning a farm girl into a billionaire's wife hadn't changed her spending habits.

"I thought you wore some on your wedding day."

"Doesn't count. They were my something borrowed from one of my old roommates. Now, which is it going to be? Getting to see you smile, dancing along the banks of the Seine or me with a frown because the new shoes pinch my feet?"

Outside the window, a black service car pulled up to the curb. Gina recognized the driver. "Sebastian is here. I should leave."

Zoe reached over and grabbed Gina's bullet journal. "I'll hold this hostage until I get an answer."

Gina slipped on her coat. "I think Nick is here."

"Oh! Take my to-go box. I'm supposed to have lunch with him, and I can't do that with the remains of brunch here. We've only been here for two and a half hours." Zoe set her box on top of Gina's. "Shoes or Paris?"

Gina stood at the end of the booth and gathered her bag and boxes and leaned over the table, reaching for the journal.

Zoe held up the blue journal near the window. "Shoes or Paris? Please don't make my feet hurt."

"Fine, Paris. But I'll make you walk so far you'll wish you'd bought the shoes instead." Gina snatched the journal from Zoe and whirled around, intent on leaving before Nick arrived at the table.

She took one step and hit a wall.

André wrapped his arms around the woman to keep her from falling, something squishing against his chest as he did so.

The woman stepped back, eyes wide. "I'm so sorry." She used her hand to wipe the front of his coat as a box fell at his feet. "I—"

Nick's hand, full of paper napkins, appeared between them. "Here."

André reached for them at the same time as the woman did, and when their fingers touched, she jumped back, colliding with the table. A book and another box fell at their feet, whipping cream and strawberries exploding from the box.

"My journal!" The woman bent to retrieve the book as André stepped out of harm's way. No telling what this unbalanced woman would destroy next. A waitress appeared with a damp towel and handed it to André. He blotted the cream and strawberries off his coat, hoping the hotel's dry-cleaning service worked weekends. The waitress handed the woman another towel. She wiped at the mess on her open coat and sweater.

Nick sat down in the booth next to a woman who must be his wife, Zoe, considering Nick held her hand. The woman—Zoe's boss, he guessed—looked at them, a deep blush coloring her cheeks.

Nick took André and the woman's towels and set them on the table. "André, allow me to introduce Gina. André is visiting. I invited him to lunch."

Gina looked up, her brown eyes glistening. She lifted her chin as if she could hold back the tears by sheer willpower. "I apologize again. I'll pay for the dry cleaning."

Hoping to set her at ease, André exaggerated his accented English. "*Non, mademoiselle*. It is my fault. Besides, every Frenchman's dream is to have a beautiful American woman throw herself at him the first time they meet, n'est-ce pas? A cleaning bill is not much to pay for a dream come true."

Gina blinked, and the threatening tears retreated. She gave him a wobbly smile. "I doubt your dream includes having crêpes smeared on your coat."

"Then I owe you crêpes."

She shook her head. "No, thank you. I was just leaving. Enjoy your lunch." She turned to Nick and his wife. "I'll see you later."

"Don't you dare back out, or I'll buy you three pairs of shoes." Nick's wife winked.

Gina nodded and stepped around André. Was the electricity he'd felt at their earlier touch something more than static? He stopped her with a hand on her shoulder. "You missed a spot." Using his thumb, he wiped a speck of cream from her chin. Her breath caught, and she blushed again as she tucked a dark curl behind her ear. It was the blush of a rose this time, not of deep embarrassment. Definitely not static. His gaze followed her out the door before turning back to the table.

"I would like you to meet my wife, Zoe. Zoe, this is André Batiste."

Zoe nodded. "So nice to meet you. I guess I should admit half the food was mine. I hadn't realized how late we were."

"And you were sending the evidence home with Gina? As if Sebastian bringing us here to Lucinda's instead of the restaurant we agreed on wasn't evidence enough." Nick looked at his wife with an intensity that made André wish for a menu to divert his attention.

Zoe shook her head a fraction and turned to André. "Gina isn't usually—" She waved her hand at the scene of the crime. "Right, Nick?" Zoe beamed at her husband. Honey wasn't as sweet.

Gina had been right to rush out of the restaurant. Newlyweds believed bliss should be contagious. The way Nick and Zoe gazed at each other, they probably wanted to share with him. André hoped to change the conversation from focusing on anything resembling matchmaking. "Nick claims you have never been to Paris but plans to rectify that lapse in two weeks."

"I am so excited, even if he has business there."

"I've promised only two days."

"That is okay. I talked Gina into going to Paris too."

André noticed the look of horror that fleetingly passed over Nick's face.

Zoe patted his arm. "Don't worry, she is not staying with us or anything. Paris is on her bucket list, and she needs a vacation. I told her we could go to the museums together while you were in meetings. She doesn't enjoy being around newlyweds any more than the rest of our friends."

Present company included.

Zoe turned back to André. "I think newlyweds make you uncomfortable too. So, tell me what brings you to New York?"

"I am the senior vice president of Galli-Batiste International, over our North American and Asian business. I am scouting a location for a New York store and satellite office."

"Did you find the property you wanted?"

"I did, then your husband talked me out of my choice and into a better one that is less expensive."

"You should feel lucky. He is usually trying to get me to spend more money than I intend." Zoe tapped her chin. "Galli-Batiste...I know I have heard of it. Oh, it's one of those designers Nick's sisters are always trying to get me to try."

"When you are in Paris, I will get you an appointment with one of our clothiers. An experience to remember, I am told. Perhaps you can bring your friend Gina. Even the most devoted of husbands prefers not to be shopping for long."

Nick smiled. "My wife is not like most women. Once she looks at a price tag, she'll be out of there and looking for a store that doesn't require an appointment."

"Then we shall make sure she doesn't see a price tag." André held back a laugh after studying Zoe's face and realizing her husband told the truth. He'd doubted Nick's earlier claim that his wife wasn't after him for the money, but her unoriginal sweater and swat at her husband's arm told him Nick had been lucky enough to not only marry a good woman, but for love.

A monster of jealousy jumped up and down inside him, yelling about the inequities of life. If he had married for love, would he feel so guilty about his wife's death?

Gina shut down her computer. Her phone pinged. Zoe again.

—Sebastian will be there in five.

Had she forgotten anything? She needed to tell—

Ping!

— Shut the door and leave the building. Trust your designers.

Gina reached for the laptop case. Ping.

—Stop! Put the laptop back. No working on vacation.

How does she know?

—I'm serious. I'll drop it in the Atlantic midflight.

April knocked on the door. "Zoe says to get out to the car and that if you have your laptop, I am to rip the bag off your body. And if you miss the seven-thirty flight to Paris, she will buy four pairs of shoes, whatever that means."

"Fine, I am going." Gina pointed to the laptop. "Leaving it here."

"Have fun in Paris. Find a guy to kiss on the Eiffel Tower. They have a spot."

Gina waved at April and grabbed her rolling suitcase from the corner. Ever since Gina told her staff she was taking a vacation, an announcement that had been met with applause, April had regaled her with stories of her own trip to Paris. The spot on the Eiffel Tower where "Place to Kiss" was painted on the floor was mentioned daily. If April wasn't such a good designer, Gina would suggest a new career as a romance author.

No way was she kissing a stranger, not even in Paris. The face of the man she'd spilled crêpes all over flashed in her mind. Nope, not even Nick's friend with the enchanting accent.

As Gina exited the office tower, Sebastian pulled into the drop-off area. The Gooding's driver took her bag and opened the door of the black limo. Nick and Zoe sat inside. Zoe clapped her hands. "Told you it would work."

Gina sat in the rear-facing seat. "What would work?"

"Texting that you had five minutes when you had ten. You almost brought the laptop, too, didn't you?"

"No comment."

"Here is your ticket and hotel reservation. The Astotel is not too big and about what you would pay in Indiana, and breakfast and teatime are included. And it's located only a block and a half from the apartment." Zoe handed Gina an envelope.

Gina recalled the hotel from the bargain travel websites she'd looked at during her free time. It met their agreement on price. The ticket presented a problem. "This says business, not coach."

"I want you to get some sleep. We arrive at eight in the morning. Besides, Nick and I are in premiere class, and you are on the same plane—all part of the deal. Plus, with that ticket, you can hang out with us in the lounge while we wait for the plane and go through the quick TSA lines." Zoe bounced in her seat.

Gina caught Nick's eye. "Has she been this excited all week?"

"You should have seen her dancing around the penthouse when her passport arrived."

Zoe jabbed Nick with her elbow. "It is my first passport. You and Gina already had two."

Nick held up five fingers. Naturally, he'd probably visited Europe before he turned five giving him three passports before his eighteenth birthday.

"I only used the old one to go to Canada," said Gina.

Nick handed Gina a water bottle and raised his own. "Here's to two weeks of fun."

Gina raised her bottle in salute.

Zoe smiled. "Here's to bucket lists!"

Gina sat back and watched the city pass by. Her phone pinged. April had sent an image of a pink-painted circle with the words *Place to Kiss*. If she had April's sense of adventure, she would add that picture to her bucket list.

André's internal clock disagreed with his watch. The sunshine agreed with his watch, but his body wanted to hit the snooze button since it was an hour until dawn in the States. André set his bag down inside the door to his Paris apartment. Fresh flowers filled the vase in the entry hall. Grand-mère must have given his housekeeper special instructions. The quickest way to get his body to agree with his watch was to live in the correct time zone, meaning no nap. The first person André wished to see was his grandmother. Opting out of the metro, André walked the two blocks to the nearest entrance as another way to stay awake. A half hour later, he was ringing the door of Grand-mère's sixteenth-century apartment on Avenue Henri Martin. Marie, his grandmother's longtime housekeeper-friend-pretty-much-everything, answered the door. "André! The spring flowers told you to come, didn't they? One must be in Paris in the spring."

André kissed the gray-haired woman on the cheek. "Of course they did. Where is she?"

"In the parlor, waiting for you."

Parlor was a misnomer. He assumed that two hundred years ago, this section of the mansion would have been the ballroom. Doric columns topped with carved angels soared to a ceiling two stories high. Other carvings adorned the room. Balconies looked over the parlor from three sides of the second floor. The high ceiling portrayed the fate of some Greek demigod who worked out at some otherworldly gym. The gold-painted woodwork stood out against cream doors and walls. Grand-mère had decorated in her favorite shade of rose. Whenever he visited, André felt like he'd slipped back in time, to before automobiles and even trains. He half expected his grand-mère's hair to be powdered and for there to be hoops under her skirt. Instead, Grand-mère sat on the divan, scrolling through her tablet.

Before she could rise, André swooped down and kissed her on each cheek. "I have missed you so! How is my favorite girl?"

She raised one expertly penciled eyebrow. "If this is how you treat your favorite girl, it is no wonder you are single. Four months without a visit is too long. That video thing you do on the tablet is not the same."

"*Je suis désolé*. I should come to Paris more often." He was sorry for Grand-mère's sake.

"Accept your father's offer and you can be here full-time. And he can stop trying to wait me out."

André sat in the nearest chair. "Whatever do you mean?"

"His offer to take over as president. It is time. His doctor says his heart is not as healthy as mine. Mathieu is ready to retire."

"I hear cousin Arabelle— "

"Half cousin." Grand-mère had little use for his uncle's third— or was it fourth?—wife and her daughter. The woman had had the nerve to change her last name to Benoit-Galli, although his uncle had never adopted her.

"Arabelle, despite her last name, is doing a first-rate job of continuing the legacy. I couldn't design a white T-shirt with our logo on the front if I tried. I have no talent for it."

Grand-mère's crystal laugh filled the room. "You have believed the lies far too long. Once, your designs rivaled your mother's and even mine. But you listen to the wrong voices. Justine convinced you bland was chic and beautiful, and you moved to the chrome-and-black apartment where you were never happy. Your father tells you more money will be the answer and pushes you to get an MBA in the States. Your underlings tell you of your brilliance. Women tell you of your handsome face." Grand-mère tilted her head. "Perhaps that one is not a lie if you would shave that scruff off your face. . ."

André opened his mouth.

"You need to stop listening to them with your ears and listen to your heart." She jabbed a finger in his direction. "You must find your passion. I am not just talking about love. Heaven knows it is wrong for a Parisian to go so long without love. The sole reason for the creation of this room was to bring a man to love, if not a bit of lust." She poured and took a sip of the drink Marie set out. "Your father thinks you mourn Justine, but you feel guilt and betrayal, non? She flirted with everyone, including you. To be faithful, one cannot be shackled to someone they don't love, no matter how good the merger. Don't frown. Your relationship was a merger, not a marriage. You need the love you never had, but even more, you need a passion for life. Passion will make your work and life better. You must find your heart."

Justine, while a friend, was never meant to be his wife. Three days into their honeymoon to the Caribbean, he'd found her flirting with the bellboy. He'd overlooked her flirtations only to have them escalate.

"*Mon trésor*, what happened was not your fault. She got into the car with an intoxicated man who happened to be sick. A man who was not you. Why? I have no answer, but I have known many women like her who never grow up to realize love is more than just the game some play. She loved to see you jealous, your blood boiling, claiming her as yours. Every woman wants to feel *l'amour*, passion, and adoration. Justine only could feel adoration when she saw your jealousy. She never recognized the joys of being cherished and trusted." She fell silent and leaned back against her cushion.

André wondered if Grand-mère had spent most of the last four months preparing to tell him this. "You are right. We didn't have a marriage, not as you had with Grand-père. Once, I saw him just before he kissed you. In his eyes you weren't eighty. I was only a teen and had not experienced my first kiss, but I knew that what you had was special."

"*Mon amour* always saw me as he did the day we first met, before the war, before the underground. I could have become a hard woman because of the war, but he reminded me who I was in my heart. You must find and listen to your heart. Only then will you be whole." She closed her eyes and before long was asleep.

Marie bustled in from whatever alcove she'd been eavesdropping from, a shawl over her arm. "She sleeps more often now. Come back tomorrow around ten. Tell her you will search for your heart. You will both be happier."

André let himself out of the apartment and walked west, to Bois de Boulogne. He wandered through the park until he reached the lake. Only a few people had rented boats. As a child he'd pestered Grand-père to rent one so they could glide over the water. If the lake was not too crowded, he would have his wish, and Grand-père would hand the boat master his fee. They'd spend the afternoon discussing the clouds in the sky and the ducks on the water as they rowed along. Once, he'd brought Justine on a picnic to the boat dock, but the boats were too dirty and her dress too white.

He wandered until he found a metro and headed back to his apartment as dusk fell over the city.

The suitcase near the door tripped him. He saw the apartment as his grand-mère had described it. Too harsh, too clean, too cold. He longed to return to Grand-mère's and curl up in her spare room, where its gilded angels would bless his sleep. Instead, he fell into a white bed with white sheets and spent dream after dream searching for the heart Grand-mère claimed he'd lost.

As the captain announced their final approach, Gina's body told her the time was closer to 2:00 a.m. than 8:00 a.m. despite the in-flight breakfast. The business section's cocoon-like seats had provided an excellent night's slumber, or partial night's sleep— better than she would have gotten in coach squished between two passengers she'd never met before. A private window seat with no other passengers to make small talk! She only imagined what first-class offered.

Before tucking her bullet journal into the antitheft crossbody bag she'd splurged on for the trip—a silly purchase considering she was just as likely to be pickpocketed in her own city—Gina checked her plan for the day. If it was sunny, she would walk the Champs-Élysées from L'Arc de Triomphe to the Louvre and back. If it was rainy, she would stop at the Place de la Concorde and return the way she had come, exploring as many shops as she could. She wondered if she could check in early or at least leave her bag at the hotel. Walking so far with a suitcase behind her would be annoying.

She found Zoe and Nick waiting for her at the end of the Jetway. They waited in the customs line together. The rectangular stamp inked in her passport appeared nothing like the stamp in her dreams. Only a small *F* in a circle on the left corner indicated she'd entered France and not some other European country. They found their luggage and driver.

Nick stifled a yawn. "I doubt you can check in this early. You are welcome to come to the apartment and leave your bags, take a shower or whatever."

"Thanks, I was worried what I would do with them. But I won't stay long. This is your vacation. Paris is for lovers and all that." Gina smiled and looked out the window, not wanting to miss a single sight, even if it was only the French freeway.

"What are your plans for the day?" asked Zoe.

"The sun is shining, and I am taking full advantage of the day and walking from L'Arc to the Louvre and back."

"Just thinking about walking makes me tired." Zoe leaned on her spouse's shoulder.

"It is about seven kilometers. Not even five miles. I do that each morning on the treadmill."

Nick put his arm around Zoe. "How do you know the distance?"

Gina pulled her bullet journal out. "Paris has been on my bucket list for years. I have most of the next week planned out, with some time left to be spontaneous."

"You can't plan spontaneous!" Zoe sat up. "The definition includes 'not planned.'"

"What are your plans for dinner?" Nick pulled his wife back to his shoulder.

"I was going to spontaneously choose a place near the L'Arc de Triomphe." Gina tucked her book back in the bag.

"I know of a place. We'll meet you at six on the corner of Avenue de Fryland."

Zoe looked at the map app on her phone. "I think you mean Friedland."

"Yes, but the name reminds me of french fries." Nick smiled.

"I'll get dinner on my own. This is your vacation. I will make myself scarce."

"You'll need to come back to the apartment to get your suitcase anyway. If you are with us, you need not wonder if you are interrupting our plans."

Zoe blushed at her husband's comment.

Gina hid a smile. "Fine. I'll spontaneously meet you at the Arc."

Their driver navigated a narrow street and parked in front of a pale stone building closely resembling the others they'd passed. They exited the car, and the driver handed them their bags. Gina took her first deep breath of Parisian air.

André's phone rang just after dawn. Sitting up in bed, he answered it. "Bonjour, Père."

"You didn't call when you got in yesterday."

"No, I visited Grand-mère and then went to bed early." His stomach rumbled, reminding him that other than the light snack Marie had prepared, he hadn't eaten.

"Come have breakfast with me and we can talk. I have much to tell you."

André kept silent. After his grand-mère's slip yesterday, he could imagine.

"André?"

"Sorry, I need time to clean up."

"I'll see you in an hour." The call disconnected.

André stumbled into the bathroom. His heart hadn't appeared in any of his dreams. One thing for sure—his passion didn't lie in the offices above the store on the Champs-Élysées or the modern studio where designers competed to make a name for themselves while pretending fidelity to the Galli-Batiste brand. He no longer wished to design. Ever.

He sent a text to Marie, hoping she still slept. **Père called. I'll come as soon as I can. Need to go see him.** *But probably not today.*

He couldn't text what Grand-mère and Marie would both assume.

— Elinore says to "follow your heart."

His heart? He had no idea if it was even still there. Not wanting to discuss that in a text he gave a short reply.

I'll try.

The sidewalk cleared as other tourists sought shelter from the falling rain. Gina pulled her polka-dot umbrella from her purse and continued walking. There was something sad about the number of American stores there were in Paris. As much as she loved the iconic mouse, the themed children's store seemed out of place, as did the hamburger chains and other stores so familiar to her. No way would she go into any of them, not even to avoid the rain. One did not fly all night to find everything the same as in her own city. Clothing companies found in any mall in the States also dotted the street. Gina focused on the architecture, determined not to allow the very un-Parisian stores to ruin her day.

By the time she reached the Place de la Concorde, the rain had slowed to a pleasant drizzle, allowing her an unobstructed view of the Egyptian obelisk. She closed her eyes and imagined a guillotine with her favorite fictional hero, the Scarlet Pimpernel, swooping in to save some distressed lady whose only crime was to have been born to a life far more comfortable than most. She checked her phone, not believing her body to know the time. Regardless of what the numbers on the display said, her stomach told her it was time for food. Unsure if she would find any vendors in the park, and unwilling to return without reaching her planned destination, Gina dug a protein bar out of the bottom of her purse. Like most bars of its class, it tasted much the same as if a toddler made a sandwich of cardboard and peanut butter and then drizzled the entire thing with chocolate-flavored wax. Gina should know as of late. The bar had become her go-to at lunch-time so she could save her lunch money for this trip, where she was still eating them. She walked around the octagon-shaped pool before continuing down the wide tree-lined path to the Louvre.

When the sun peeked out from behind the clouds, Gina shook out her umbrella, then folded it and hung it from her bag. Light danced off the wet leaves. Gina attempted two artistic photos with her phone before the screen flashed a red warning. Low battery? How was that possible? She'd charged the phone all night on the plane. A few steps later, she couldn't resist pulling out her phone for another photo. She passed each sculpture, admiring the work. Only a handful of passersby did the same. Suddenly, two weeks was far too little time to take all of Paris in. Did the locals care about the amazing city they lived in, or was the city something they dutifully walked past on school trips?

The Louvre stood larger than she'd imagined. Too bad she hadn't studied art history and chosen the summer-abroad option. At the time, she didn't think she would rue her choice. Now she added it to her list of regrets. The one list she didn't keep in her bullet journal.

A street hawker tried to sell her five Eiffel Tower key chains for a euro. Despite his pitch, Gina was sure she would find the same deal all over the city. She wandered back, taking a different route, past a tree with a trunk well over three feet in diameter. If trees could talk, the stories this one would tell. As a young sapling, it may have stood tall for Napoleon. She looked at her phone. The screen remained dim but was bright enough to tell her she'd dawdled longer than she intended. Gina put her phone into the battery conservation mode. Even then she only had just over an hour of power left. Just enough time to meet Zoe and Nick for Dinner. Gina picked up her pace and returned in the Arc's direction.

Just as she was passing the first shops of the Champs-Élysées, the buildings to her left began swirling inside a halo only she could see. *No! Not now. I'm on vacation.* She bumped into someone.

"Pardon."

"Pardon."

Benches. There were benches along here. Gina clutched her cross-body bag tighter, covered her right eye, and turned in a slow circle. An unoccupied bench sat between two trees. She made her way to the bench, aware that people were stepping around her. Walking with more than half her vision obscured was difficult. She probably looked like a drunken tourist.

At the bench, she pulled out her phone and dialed Zoe's number. Four rings and her call went to voice mail. "It's Gina. I have one of my headaches, and my phone is dying. I'm just past the Roosevelt Met—"

After three beeps, her phone died completely. Gina stared at it. The halo made the screen shimmer and bounce. Panic bubbled up inside her. If she was at home, she could call an Uber. Cancel that. She couldn't call anyone. Gina bit her lip. L'Arc de Triomphe stood at least nearly a kilometer away. Maybe Zoe would get the message and come looking for her. However, that might not be until she was late to their meeting point. Gina closed her eyes and rubbed her temples, not that her head hurt, but maybe the massage would help with the ocular migraine like with a real headache. It didn't. She opened her eyes to orient herself. There were enough pedestrians that she shouldn't have a problem crossing the streets as long as she stayed with a group. Not knowing if there was someone on her right side and running into them would be the most difficult part. She stood and took two steps to her right. Her foot caught on a crack in the sidewalk and threatened to topple her onto her face.

She turned to walk back to her bench and bumped into a pedestrian instead. "Pardon."

The pedestrian didn't move. "*Êtes-vous blessée?*" a deep voice said in French.

It took Gina a moment to translate what the stranger had said and to form a coherent lie that nothing was wrong. The man could be a pickpocket or worse. "*Il n'en est rien.*"

"You are American?" he replied in barely accented English.

Gina nodded and stepped back.

He put a hand on her shoulder. "Careful. You nearly collided with a stroller." His hand slid down her shoulder and cupped her elbow. "Are you in trouble? Lost?"

A stranger's touch should bring her fear, but instead she found comfort. Gina struggled with what to tell him. It wasn't wise to tell a strange man she was temporarily blind. "I'm not lost, just having a difficult time —I mean, I was going to meet my friends."

"I think we have met before."

Impossible.

Gigi? Nina? André was sure he'd run into this woman before in New York. No two women could possess such a glorious mass of curls. Yet she expressed no spark of recognition. "Perhaps I met your twin—a woman who ran into me in New York City only—"

The woman gasped. She stared at him, though not exactly at his face—more at his ear. "In a restaurant?"

"Oui, she had crêpes in a box."

She blushed then. Definitely the same woman. "I'm so sorry—"

"Non, I am flattered you came all this distance to throw yourself into my arms again ...Jenny?"

Her blush deepened. He knew he shouldn't tease her even if a woman whose blushes remained unpracticed intrigued him.

"Close. Gina. And you are Mr. Galli-Batiste?"

"No, I am André Batiste. Galli is the name of my maternal grandparents."

Her gaze remained unfocused, yet she didn't smell of wine or alcohol.

"Now that you remember me, I must ask again, is something wrong?"

"It is rather difficult to explain, but in my case, the term "blinding headaches" is literal. I tried to call Nick and Zoe Gooding to tell them of my plight, but my phone died. I took far too many photos today." She held up her phone, her gaze someplace in the middle of his chest.

André guided her to a bench. "Sit for a moment. I am assuming your friends are in the city?"

"We flew in this morning. I mean, we were on the same plane. I'm not on vacation with them. That would be weird." She shuddered.

"I am glad to know even American newlyweds are smart enough not to bring friends on a honeymoon to Paris."

"Yes, but I couldn't check into my hotel, so I left my suitcase at Nick's apartment. We are eating dinner together, and then I will get my things."

"I see. But you cannot walk to your meeting place without bumping into people or strollers. And your friends do not know where you are. Perhaps I can help." He pulled out his phone.

Nick answered on the second ring. "André?"

"Hello. I understand you are in Paris."

"I was going to call you on Monday. How did you know?"

André studied Gina, who seemed to be concentrating on the sidewalk at her feet. "I ran into your lovely friend, or, rather, she ran into me."

"You found Gina?" Nick's next words were muffled. "Zoe is so thankful. I don't know if Gina explained, but she can't see well at the moment. We were going to meet her near the Arc on the corner of Fry—"

"Friedland"

"Yes, there. Can you help her get there? We are still en route. Perhaps you could join us for dinner."

"Oui. I can do that."

"Thank you. We will be there in twenty minutes."

"So will we." André ended the call. "Nick told me where to meet them. Do you mind if I escort you?"

Gina raised her head and looked in his general direction. "I suffer from ocular migraines. They disturb my vision. It should fade away in a few more minutes. Already my left eye seems to be calming down."

André held out his arm, but she didn't move. "In case you cannot see it, I'm extending my hand." Gina set her hand in his. The same electric shock he'd felt in the restaurant ran up his arm. Could he offer to show her around Paris without it sounding like the pickup line it was?

"May I have you walk on my right side? I see nothing out of my right eye, and I am in danger of running into all sorts of things."

He moved her hand to the crook of his elbow. "But of course. A gentleman must always walk between the lady and the street."

"My father told my brother the same thing."

André stopped at the cross street. "What did you do on your first day in Paris?"

"I walked from the Arc to the Louvre."

"Alone?"

"There are far too many tourists to be alone."

"You did not bring a boyfriend with you?"

She shook her head.

"Grand-mère says Paris is for lovers. A beautiful woman should not be alone in Paris in the spring."

Another blush crept up her cheeks. André wondered if she was unused to the compliments or embarrassed about being alone. "I suppose it was your grandmother who taught you how to flirt with American women?"

André laughed. "No, mon grand-père, I watched how he treated Grand-mère and learned all I needed to know. How long will you be in Paris?"

"Two weeks." She turned and squinted in his direction.

"Do your eyes hurt?"

"No." She used her free hand to cover one eye, then the other. "My left eye is clearing up. The migraine creates halos and colors things, like watching the world through the northern lights. Have you ever seen them?"

"No, but I put them on my bucket list." Not that he had time.

"Me too, but Paris was first."

"When I was young, I wanted to see New York. It was in all the American shows."

"Was it what you expected?"

"I'm not sure. Every time I have been there, I've been on business, and the boardrooms all look the same. Last time I visited was to find real estate for a storefront and East Coast offices. So hopefully soon I will be the tourist, at least on weekends."

"If you need a tour guide …I mean …Sounds like a pickup line, doesn't it?"

"I thought the same thing a few moments ago when I wanted to ask if you wanted a guide for Paris. But then I remembered I owed you some crêpes. I thought I'd use them to see you again instead."

"I think your guiding me up the Champs-Élysées is more than enough; after all, the crêpes on your clothing was my fault."

"You are in Paris. You must have crêpes." The hold on his arm loosened. "Are you feeling better?"

"Despite the name 'head*ache*,' they don't hurt. But I can discern more with each step. Unfortunately, the stores I see are the same as those in New York. I think out of reverence for the architecture, they should have renamed that restaurant *Cinq Garçons*."

"Five boys. *Cinq Gars* would be closer. Grand-mère would agree with you as she also thinks Paris has become too American. On behalf of my country, my apologies."

"If it makes you feel better, I refuse to go into any store or restaurant I know is American."

"But in New York you have French restaurants and even French stores. Isn't that the same?"

"I guess I am just so used to it. I can buy food from every country in the world in New York."

"The same in Paris, but I admire your pledge to avoid American. Perhaps I should speak only French."

"Then you would have to endure my college French, and that could be awful."

"*Terrible*." He pronounced the word in French.

"One thing I love about the French language is that even bad things sound good in it." She stopped and loosened her hold on his arm. She covered one eye and then the other. "I can almost see again."

André tucked her hand back into his arm. "You would not deprive me of escorting you the rest of the way, would you?"

"No, I can add this to my adventure list. My friends will be jealous when I tell them I had a handsome Parisian flirting with me as I walked down the Champs-Élysées."

How jealous could he make her friends in the next two weeks?

The hazy gray fog in Gina's right eye had lingered. After nearly tipping her glass over, she didn't dare reach for her water again. The dim lighting of the restaurant didn't help matters. She duplicated Zoe's order when the words of the menu refused to come into focus. Unfortunately, the entrée came drowned in a delicious sauce. Not spilling on anyone, especially André, became the focus of her meal. The lighthearted banter they'd shared on the walk faded as the dinner progressed. André's seductive accent mesmerized her as he told them stories of his favorite places to visit.

"It is the same in New York? Tourists stay in certain areas? When I was in high school I made it a game to see if I could avoid spotting a tourist the entire day." Gina had learned when she arrived in New York fresh out of college a decade ago that some tourists blended in better than others.

"I still feel like a sightseer in NYC half the time, but I haven't even lived there for a year. The best part about this trip is I can be a tourist without having a bodyguard watching every move." Zoe smiled and dove into her meal. Nick raised a brow at André.

Gina pretended to take a drink while she looked at the other diners in the restaurant, wondering which ones were on duty. No way would Nick let Zoe tour the world unguarded after the mess last fall. One or two especially fit tourists were candidates. Lowering her glass, Gina hesitated momentarily, wondering where to set it down. Distance became an elusive measurement as her eyes readjusted. She concentrated on the spot she was sure the glass needed to go. Millimeters from her target, Zoe's voice interrupted her concentration. "Does Tuesday work for you, Gina?"

The bottom of the glass hit the rim of her plate, but André's hand shot out and covered hers, keeping it from spilling. Disaster avoided. He kept his hand over hers after she safely released the glass at the spot André guided her hand to. Once her hand was back in the safe zone and no longer over the table, he let go, like a mother guiding an errant toddler. Gina nodded her thanks, hoping her shame didn't show on her face. "Sorry, Zoe, what was the question?"

"André offered to give us an appointment-only shopping experience and a tour of Galli-Batiste Tuesday afternoon."

She might be able to afford a scarf—if she found a grocery store and more protein bars and the clothiers didn't throw her out after taking one look at her bargain-basement shoes and realize she had no sense of fashion. "Sounds like fun."

André pulled out his phone. "Pardon me while I get you on the calendar." He put his phone back. "I booked you at fifteen hundred, so if you come at fourteen, I'll show you around the studio."

Zoe tapped Gina's arm. "Don't you need to check your book? I know you had plans."

Not in front of André. He already thinks I'm odd. The illustrated planner and diary would only confirm that opinion. "I'm good. I told you I had time built in for spontaneous adventures, and an appointment-only showing at one of Paris's premiere designers counts."

"You plan time to be spontaneous? Perhaps my grasp of English is not as good as I thought."

Nick laughed. "It isn't your translation. Gina has her time well organized, including when she can be spontaneous."

"Then perhaps Gina needs a dictionary." She wasn't sure whether his tone was condescending or reassuring.

Gina pulled out her bullet journal as her only defense and flipped to the pages she'd used to plan her vacation. "I wrote many things on sticky notes so I can rearrange." She pulled the note off Tuesday, moving the paper back to Monday. She put Monday morning on Tuesday morning and penned in "14:00—Galli-Batiste."

"See? All taken care of." Gina shoved her book back in her bag before André or Zoe could read her plans. They would not be as easy to reorganize as the papers she'd moved. Once she settled in her hotel room, she'd move things more efficiently.

Gina looked out of the corner of her eye at the handsome Frenchman. Only an hour ago she'd entertained the idea of a vacation romance. But that would require a whole new degree of spontaneity. André was so far out of her league. Even if she over-looked being treated like a child, which had probably saved the entire table from disaster, they came from two different worlds. Only one couple in a billion had made a relationship between two people from such different economic backgrounds work, and those two people sat across the table. After Tuesday, she would never see André again. It was all for the best. She couldn't do anything stupid, like kiss him on the Eiffel Tower or the banks of the Seine, if he wasn't there.

The yawning started during dessert. Nick attempted to hide behind his napkin. Gina did the same.

Nick checked his watch. "Perhaps we should call it a night."

"My car is parked not too far from here. Would you like a lift to the apartment?" It would be a tight squeeze in the small vehicle he used to get around Paris. However, the thought of Gina walking alone at night when he was not entirely sure she'd fully recovered from her headache worried him.

Zoe covered another yawn with her hand. "Thank you. Would you mind dropping Gina at the hotel after you drop us off at the apartment? She hasn't checked in yet and we have her suitcases."

"I can walk—"

"No problem." André cut off Gina's protest. They covered the two blocks to where André had left his car, Gina walking stiffly beside him. Behind him, Nick wrapped his arm around Zoe.

Nick commented on his car first. "I expected your car to be bigger."

"Perfect size for Paris. Easy in and out of traffic. Fits in our minuscule parking spaces. Your American cars would never do for some of our narrower streets." The four-year-old dented Citroën provided the perfect cover. No one would guess a billionaire drove such a normal car, and he detested bodyguards more than the unobservant Zoe.

"It is charming—like a baby car." Zoe slid into the back seat, Nick in tow.

André navigated through the Saturday-evening traffic to the address Nick gave him. "Nice location. How did you find this flat?"

"My father bought the place for my mother years ago. As long as our plans don't conflict with hers, my sisters and I are welcome to use it whenever we wish."

André parked a few doors away and accompanied the group to the apartment. Although his family did not deal in real estate, he was always interested to learn how architects divided and repurposed the old buildings. The Gooding's apartment was on the third floor. Original woodwork adorned the entryway. Gina and Zoe exchanged hugs and whispered plans.

Nick pulled André aside. "Thank you for rescuing Gina tonight. Zoe was beside herself worrying we could never find her. Glad to see you before our business meeting this week." André shook Nick's hand.

Gina held a pink-handled polka-dot suitcase in her hand.

"Is this all of your luggage?" At Gina's nod, André reached for the bag. "Then you must allow me." For a moment, he thought she would argue with him. Instead, she let go of the handle and stepped away. One final goodbye and they were out on the landing.

"We can take the elevator. The sign claims it holds eight people, but how would they fit unless they were all circus performers." Gina pointed to the small door next to the stairs.

"Being a contortionist is a talent all Europeans share—so we can fit in our cars."

Her laugh was mellow, not the high-pitched, fake giggle so many women used. "Can the thing hold the two of us and a suitcase? Or would you rather take the stairs?"

"I am not sure. I've been gone from Paris so long I've forgotten how to contort myself to fit in an elevator with a pretty woman."

She blushed and tucked her hair behind her ear. Since dinner, her face had lost the tenseness that had grown throughout their meal. Gina opened the narrow elevator door. "Let's chance it. I'd rather not have you fall down the stairs with my suitcase."

André guided the two of them and the roller bag into the cramped space. Gina stood on tiptoe to leave extra floorspace. Standing that way, she was the right height to be kissed. André banished the notion. He was not one for short-term relationships. The elevator squeaked as it descended to ground level, stopping with a jerk.

"Perhaps next time it would be safer to take the stairs." Gina held open the door for him as he maneuvered the suitcase out of the narrow doorway.

André put her suitcase in the back seat. "Which way to your hotel?"

Gina pointed down the street. "About two blocks over and one down."

André held open the door for her, and she slid into the passenger seat. He rounded the car and got in but didn't start the engine. "I'd like to ask for your phone number. Normally I'd give you mine, but since your phone is dead, I'll text you mine. If you have another headache, call me. I'm in Paris most of the month." He handed Gina his phone, open to an empty contact page.

She hesitated a moment before she typed in her number. "Thank you so much for your help today. I can't believe my luck running into you, of all the people in Paris."

"I must admit it wasn't entirely an accident. I saw you sitting on the bench as I exited the store, and you reminded me so much of yourself I had to see who your doppelgänger was. When you ran into me, I was walking up to meet you."

The light of the streetlamp illuminated her smile. "You were looking for me?"

"I wanted you to take me up on my offer to get you crêpes."

As Gina handed him back the phone, their fingers touched for the space of the breath. Just long enough to send an electric spark straight to his heart, speeding it up. "I'm surprised after this evening you would admit you wanted to meet me again. I am destined to be one disaster after another."

"I hope I did not embarrass you too much with the water glass. It seems your eyesight was not as restored as you thought."

"I guess not. And the dim light in the restaurant didn't help. My eye doctor says I'm a light hog, especially when my eyes are tired. Give me one-hundred-watt bulbs and I'm happy."

"That is why you ordered the same meal as Zoe?"

"It was the easiest thing to do."

"Next time we are out, if you cannot read the menu, please ask me."

Her eyes widened. "Next time?"

André turned the ignition and drove down the street before he said, "I think there should be one, don't you?"

Orange marmalade and croissants quickly climbed to the top of Gina's favorite-foods list. Of course, they wouldn't taste as good at home. The single-serving marmalade bottle must have been dipped in a magic potion rendering it irresistible. And Parisians must go to great expense to infuse the air with the same potion. Why else would she have agreed to André's invitation for there to be a next time? At thirty-three, she knew better than to fall for a winning smile and a smooth accent. Though, admittedly, he was the first man with a French accent to express interest in her.

Even the hot chocolate tasted better in France. Gina closed her eyes and took another sip. She pulled out her bullet journal and turned to the next blank page.

My Favorite French Foods
1. Orange marmalade and croissants

Her phone pinged. She didn't recognize the number of the incoming text.

—**Bonjour, it's André. Now that you have my number, please save it and promise you will use it if you get stranded again.**

Thank you—I mean, merci.

—Can you move around your plans and fit me in at ten for two hours to experience the best crêpes in the city?

Yes.

—I will pick you up at your hotel, then.

See you then.

Flipping to today's schedule in her journal, Gina folded the paper "Walk through the Latin quarter" in half so it only took up the space for the afternoon and penned in "Crêpes with André."

Back in her room, Gina studied her reflection. If possible, her hair was curlier than normal. The jeans-and-T-shirt tourist look wouldn't do. The best crêpes in Paris were most likely not in some tiny street-side café. She traded her faded jeans for a midcalf jumper dress. The casual plaid worked with her sensible walking shoes. She extracted a sweater from her suitcase and checked her purse to make sure she had all the provisions she needed for the day, including a backup battery charger for her phone. Satisfied, Gina set off to explore the surrounding blocks while she waited for André to arrive.

A block away from Gina's hotel, André spotted a woman with short brunette curls. He slowed the car and watched as she admired the building. To his eye, there was nothing exceptional about the structure—white brick, wrought iron, and small-paned windows with a few stone flourishes about the eaves, but Gina studied the building as if she hadn't just walked past three nearly identical ones.

He rolled down the window. "Gina!"

She turned, a smile lighting her face, and hurried over to the car. André leaned over and opened the passenger door. "Sorry I didn't get out, but I am not exactly at a place to park."

Gina checked her wristwatch. "For a moment I thought I was late."

"Parking. Always best to be early when driving in Paris." André put the sports car into gear.

Gina ran her hand over the leather upholstery. "This is a step up from the car you drove yesterday."

The 1968 Blue Alpine A110 had originally been Grand-père's. Gina didn't seem to be one of those people who recognized classic French sports cars, so André gave an easier answer. "I got this car when I was much younger and wanted to impress women. The other one is practical. Who would ever believe I drive a dented Citroën with faded paint? No one has ever attempted to steal it."

"I didn't notice the faded paint last night. Is the dent real or deliberate?"

"No idea. I bought the car that way." André turned down another road leading to a bridge across the Seine.

"So your cars have logic behind them. You have an 'I'm nothing special—move on' car and a 'I'm hot stuff' car. What other cars do you have?"

A few months after he'd married Justine, he'd thought a family car would be nice. "In LA, I keep a Lexus. You could call the Lexus my 'I'm somebody, but I don't need your attention' car. What type of car do you have?"

"I don't. Parking in the city costs so much there isn't much point. I learned to drive in an old Ford Taurus. I think my parents still have it. I've rented cars on a few business trips, but I am just as happy not driving." Gina looked out the window. "It is easier to see the world when you aren't driving. When I am driving, I get too caught up on what is on the road and forget to pay attention to what I am passing."

"I think I heard something similar in a productivity seminar on the reasoning to take a vacation."

Gina turned to face him. "I didn't mean to be profound. But I guess it is a good metaphor. Sometimes work becomes my road and I never look up." She took a deep breath. "You didn't tell me what restaurant we are going to."

"We are not."

Gina stiffened. "Then where?"

"Grand-mère's. I was supposed to visit yesterday, but my father wanted to talk business and we ended up talking most of the day." More like a daylong argument. André was of the opinion his cousin Arabelle had a better fashion vision for the company. "Marie, who works for my grandmother, makes the best crêpes in the city. When she told me that is what Grand-mère wanted for brunch today after she returned from Mass, I asked if I could bring a friend."

"You are taking me to visit your grandmother? Do you normally bring random tourists to meet her?"

"Never. You are the first tourist I have ever brought to her home. You are also the first tourist to sit in this car. Unless Grand-père picked up tourists in it." André turned onto his grand-mère's street.

"This area is lovely. The groomed gardens and old buildings, are what, three or four hundred years old? Were there guards at that building back there?"

"So many questions. Yes, it's an embassy of some country that starts with a *B*. There are several embassies in the area, including the Russian. I believe Grand-mère's building dates to the sixteenth century." He pulled up to the gate protecting the drive to the garage under the building and used his remote to open it.

"Is the entire house your grandmother's?"

"Non, she has an extensive apartment, though. The building was divided into apartments more than a hundred years ago. Just wait until you see the inside."

I'm meeting his grandma! Maybe it was normal in France, but she'd only met the grandparent once after facing the parents months after the first date.

Not a date.

No dating in Paris.

No vacation romances.

André took her hand on the stairway. "Careful. Some are slick."

No electricity traveling up her arm like yesterday. *Chemistry means nothing.* André wasn't the first guy who caused a tiny spark to flare. Under the right conditions, most men could manage a spark or two, some even starting something as miraculous as fireworks on New Year's Eve, only to be outlasted by the average diet resolution when faced with words like *commitment* and *marriage.* She slipped her hand out of his when they stopped in front of a pair of white doors trimmed in gold. A woman in her late sixties opened it.

"André!"

He took her by the shoulders and placed a kiss on each cheek. "Marie, this is Gina Swann."

Marie hugged Gina and kissed her cheeks, then turned to André and spoke in French. Gina only caught a few words, but she surmised André was not in the woman's good graces. She pointed to a room through another set of double doors.

"Marie says Grand-mère is in the parlor."

"That wasn't your grandmother?"

"Non, but she has been in Grand-mère's employ for fifty years. She scolded me for not telling her how beautiful you were and for not saying more about you earlier as neither of them could concentrate during Mass."

Having only read about housekeepers or seen them in movies, Gina could form no reply. She followed him into the parlor but stopped near the entrance. No wonder André hadn't described the apartment in detail. The room was right out of a fairy-tale castle. André continued across the room to where a woman sat on a couch, and exchanged kisses with her.

"Bonjour and welcome." The older woman extended her hands and pulled Gina down to kiss her cheeks.

"Gina this is ma grand-mère, Elinore Galli."

Gina looked at André, then back to the impeccably dressed woman. "*The* Elinore Galli?" Gina smoothed her jumper, wishing she had worn something nicer. Her sensible walking shoes defiled the famous designer's home.

Elinore gestured to the couch opposite her. "André, you didn't tell her? My apologies. My grandson only sees me as his grandmother, which I appreciate very much." Her English was flawless. "I own a jumper dress exactly like yours. And find it comfortable when working in my little garden."

A gardening dress? Gina wished she'd brought something nicer. "You have a garden too? Of course you do. Your apartment is right out of a fairy tale."

"I had the same look on my face when mon Henri showed me this apartment forty years ago. After we eat, André will take you on a tour." She turned to her grandson and waited for a nod. "When my son got married, we moved here and left the house to him. I didn't want to leave the mansion for some modern history-less place where I wouldn't find any inspiration for my creations."

"Do you still design?"

"*Mais oui!*" She tapped her head. "I cannot see a woman and not think of a creation that would make her look her best. An outfit she will feel confident yet beautiful in. The young designers today all try to outdo each other and create things no real woman can wear. Women are not meant to be shaped like twelve-year-old boys, and the models all look like drug addicts!"

André leaned over and took his grandmother's hand. "This is an ongoing argument between Grand-mère and the rest of the board. Incidentally, I agree with her in many respects. Some designs presented in the summer collection would get an American woman arrested if she wore them outside her house. But let's not talk about work."

Elinore studied André. "Mathieu's offer did not go well?"

"That is still work."

Marie came in and nodded.

"Saved by the food, *mon trésor*. No more talk of work. We will eat in the kitchen." Elinore extended a hand to André for assistance. Once she was standing with her arm linked through his, she turned to Gina. "We rarely eat in the dining room as Marie hates moving the china, which is only for show."

The modern kitchen stunned Gina almost as much as the sixteenth-century house. André seated his grand-mère, then Gina. "Come, Marie. Join us. Gina won't be shocked. She is American. I see your plate on the counter."

"But the staff ..." Marie's thickly accented English trailed off as Elinore and André rolled their eyes. She moved her plate to the table and sat down in the chair André held out for her.

Elinore leaned across the table and stage whispered. "I retired her two years ago, but she won't leave. Once you taste her crêpes, you'll understand why I don't toss her out."

Milk, eggs, butter, sugar, vanilla, salt, and flour. The recipe for crêpes was as simple as they came. Until Gina took her first bite, she doubted one crêpe could taste better than another.

Gina bumped orange marmalade and croissants down to number two and put Marie's crêpes in her number-one spot on her list. "These are amazing."

Could this vacation get any better?

André hid his smile at Marie's shock to Gina's offer to help clean up. André gathered plates and moved them to the counter as Grand-mère clucked at him. He extended a hand to Gina. "Why don't I show you the rest of the apartment."

They stopped at the base of the wrought-iron circular stairway, where a few family photographs hung.

"Did I offend them?"

"Non, but you are a guest, and it is unusual for Grand-mère's guests to make such an offer." André pointed to the photos. "This is mon grand-père, Henri Galli. He used a cane most of his life, having been injured when the Germans invaded France in 1940. He and Grand-mère both participated in the French underground, which was how they met." He moved on to the next photo. "They married during the war. For their ten-year anniversary, Grand-mère designed the wedding dress she would have had if silk had been available. She made the lace with her friend's help."

Gina leaned close to the photo. "It is exquisite."

"You'll see the original on our tour Tuesday. This is my uncle and my mother. Grand-mère claims she was born designing clothes and was almost never without a scarf." André pointed to a photo taken when his mother was five and his uncle fourteen.

"I am glad this photo is not in color. The plaids and stripes don't match."

André laughed. "You are probably correct. These are my parents when they first met. Mère was just seventeen and already designing for Grand-mère. Père's family was in industry. They married a year later. Most people think the Batiste in Galli-Batiste International is for my father, but mother used her new last name immediately, and she and Grand-mère changed the name of the company."

"Then this is you as a child?"

"Non, that is my older brother, Martin. He died when he was six, before I was born. This one is me."

Gina looked from the photo to André, then back, and nodded. André followed her up the circular staircase. "This staircase must have been added when the house was divided, I can't picture any woman in heavy crinolines or hoops being able to navigate it."

"The grand staircase located outside the apartments would have been the access two years ago. There is a locked door leading back out to the staircase as well as a set of servants' stairs off the kitchen."

Gina took a few steps past the staircase to one balcony overlooking the parlor area. She stood still, mouth slightly open. André studied her. Some pretended to appreciate the ornate wood and plaster work. Gina's fascination was not feigned. He led her from room to room, allowing her time to study each painting and detail. André tried to look at the familiar through new eyes.

In the far room, Gina gasped and turned from the balcony, her cheeks flamed.

"You found our naughty angels."

"*Naughty* is one word for it."

André chuckled. The angelic lovers left little to the imagination. "I imagine over the years they have inspired many a couple to seek a private location."

"No doubt several shotgun marriages came from those alcoves as well." Gina looked out the window to the garden below.

"The building behind this one was built after World War II. There used to be a grand garden off the terrace. Now there is only a little one. Would you like to see it?" André led her to a door concealed at the end of a row of cupboards. He lifted the latch and descended first. "As a child I used to dream of this as a secret passageway some musketeer took to foil a dark plan. Imagine my disappointment to learn this is but one of many passages for the servants to move from room to room without bothering the aristocratic occupants."

"Perhaps they are the same? I could not dash a young boy's dreams."

André waited at the bottom of the stairs. Standing a stair above him, Gina's eyes were level with his and sparkled with laughter. He reached out and moved a curl behind her ear. "Every young boy dreams of rescuing a damsel in distress. I am glad I could fulfill that dream and meet you."

Her breath caught and her eyes widened. The slam of a cupboard in the kitchen around the corner stopped him from moving closer. He dropped his hand, then took hers and led her out to the small garden.

Once outside, she dropped his hand and inspected the plants. The mild spring air swirled about them, cooling André's thoughts. He'd never kissed a woman on the first date. But something about Gina made his heart beat faster and his brain stop functioning properly.

After a turn around the small area, Gina opened the door to the apartments, not waiting for him—a clear sign he'd overstepped his bounds and ruined his chance of getting to know her better.

Gina took a deep breath. André would return any second. Had he considered kissing her? Would she have kissed him back? Perhaps she should create a page in her journal for things not to do in Paris.

André closed the door behind him. "The rooms in this section are not as ornate. I suspect part of this section of the mansion may have been a service area."

She followed him through the rest of the tour. They passed two doors, which André explained were Marie's chambers, before returning to the parlor, where they resumed their seats next to his grandmother, who doodled in a notebook.

"Your home is magnificent. Thank you for allowing me to experience it. Up on the balcony, I could almost hear musicians playing the minuet and see dresses swirling on the floor below."

Elinore smiled. "I often imagined the same thing, as if the benevolent ghosts who once danced here wished to continue the party."

Gina studied the mural on the ceiling. "I am sure a few spend their days looking at everything."

"Did you take any photos?" Elinore closed the notebook.

"This is your private residence. I would never dream—"

"Well, you should. Run upstairs and take a couple. André, would you help me for a moment?"

From the balcony, Gina took three photos. She made sure she cropped out the spot where Elinore sat next to André, their heads bent over the sketchbook. Before adding a selfie to her collection, Gina checked the carved angels, making sure none were of the naughty type.

André stood, the notebook clutched in his hand, as Gina returned to the parlor. "Thank you for allowing me some photos."

"But of course. André tells me you will be in Paris for two weeks."

"As long as I dare miss work." Rather, it was as long as Adrian Scott was forcing her to take off. He had teasingly threatened to fire her if he saw her before April 15.

"Then, as my newest friend, I would like to invite you to my one-hundredth birthday party. A week from tomorrow at the Musée Rodin. It is a few days before my birthday, but the Musée rents its facilities on Monday and Tuesday mornings."

"I am honored, but we have only just met."

Elinore waved her hand at the ceiling. "But we are what I call kindred spirits. Few of my acquaintances hear the minuet during their tour. They have no imagination at all. Say you will come."

"Thank you, yes."

"André, make sure Gina gets an invitation to the dinner and the reception." She turned back to Gina. "You will be my one-hundredth friend. The problem with being this old is not only have I outlived my children, but I have outlived a few friends I planned on inviting only a month ago. I am not convinced living to be as old as Methuselah is a good thing. Now, if you will excuse me, I fear it is time for my nap. André, will you assist me?"

André walked his grand-mère in the direction of the huge bedroom Gina had glimpsed earlier. Although André insisted she could follow them in, Gina was loath to disturb the woman's privacy. Gina pulled out her bullet journal and logged the photos she had taken. She didn't hear André return until he sat down beside her.

"Do you write everything down?"

"Just things I want to remember."

"Am I in there?"

Gina pointed to the spot where she had written "Crêpes with André."

"Is that all?"

"No, I wrote a note about how you saved me last night and that it might have been a good thing. After all, had I not spilled my crêpes on you in New York, you would not have recognized me."

André pointed to her schedule. "May I see your plans for the next week?"

Gina handed the book to him.

"You can remove this one as you'll see the Musée Rodin during Grand-mère's party. If you move the pink note to Friday, I will drive you out myself." André pointed to her note to visit Chartres on Thursday.

"I shouldn't occupy so much of your time. Besides, I already purchased my ticket to the Eiffel Tower on Friday."

"May I accompany you?"

The photo of the place to kiss popped into Gina's mind, warning bells sounding. She could only handle so many near misses. His soft-blue-green eyes were far too easy to get lost in. "If you can purchase a ticket." It should be a safe answer. Last week the website indicated there were only a few left.

"At 16:30 on the second level? I will try my best." André closed her book and handed it back. "What are you doing this afternoon?"

Gina put her journal into the bag and stood to avoid his eyes as she rearranged her plans for the rest of the day. "Yes, I wanted to walk the Latin Quarter, and then I purchased a ticket on one of the tour buses for tomorrow. After four today, I can get back on the bus. The audio tour will be a good way to view everything, then choose what to go back to."

"I've never been on one of those tours."

"Of course not. People don't tour their own cities—although I went on a Duck Tour of Boston once when my cousins were visiting. But I grew up in the western part of the state." Her mouth kept blurting out words. The rambling monster had taken control. Gina bit her lip to stop it.

"You are from Massachusetts, not New York?" André walked a stair ahead of her as they descended to the garage.

"Yes, I moved to New York after I finished my schooling. I was one of the lucky ones whose internship turned into a career."

He held her door open, and Gina slipped inside. André entered from his side. "Would you like me to drop you off anyplace specific?"

Relief filled her. She hadn't known how to decline if he wanted to accompany her. And she wasn't ready to spend more time with him without analyzing the repercussions. "Any convenient corner or metro stop."

According to her phone's GPS, André had dropped her off at the north end of the Quarter. "Have a fun day. I'll see you on Tuesday. Text me if you need anything."

"Thank you for the wonderful day, and tell Marie merci. I didn't see her after our tour."

"I will." He merged back into the traffic, and the blue sports car disappeared around a corner.

The void inside chided her for not encouraging him. "Shut up. A vacation fling only works out in movies," she muttered as she walked past her first bookstore of the day.

His father had texted three times during his visit to Grand-mère's. André didn't have an answer for him yet. Not that there was much of a choice, but he'd asked Père to give him until Monday.

André took the next left turn and navigated out of the city, the little blue car eating up the miles. Soon, farms, some with ancient stone buildings, dotted the landscape. When the fields gave way to woodlands, André found a pullout and parked under the shade of several trees. He found a path that was once a road but was now blocked by a gate with a sign warning no vehicles were allowed. André hoped he'd found the place he remembered. Taking the sketchbook Grand-mère handed him and a refillable water bottle, he set off down the path.

The old moss-covered stone wall overlooked a meadow and pond. Today he was the only human to witness the view. White-and-yellow specks peppered the grass, promising flowers in the days to come. André sat on the wall and opened the book to the page Grand-mère had showed him in her parlor. He studied the design. Though she had not colored the sketch, she'd made notes along the sides, indicating fabrics and colors. In the bottom right corner, she'd signed her name, Elinore Galli, named her creation, and written down the date. At auction, the page would sell for $2,000 or $3,000. If this became the last Elinore Galli gown, which was a possibility, it would be worth ten times that. Grand-mère insisted he be the one to construct the garment. The last time he'd taken a design and turned it into clothing was the wedding dress he'd created for Justine—a dress she'd refused to wear, opting for a Versace and claiming she'd dreamed of wearing one since she was a child. His family had quietly accepted the slap in the face. Galli-Batiste had designed the rest of the clothing for the bridal party, and the wedding bloggers had a heyday noting that Galli-Batiste's newest family member found the line beneath her. Much of the Galli-Batiste wedding line, including the dress created for Justine, ended up being sold off in warehouse sales. Some unsuspecting American bride had probably worn his last gown and either sold it on Craig's list or packed it away in her attic.

Even if he wanted to sew the dress, how would he get her mea-surements? She'd sidestepped the opportunity to spend a day with him. Though the polite rebuff wasn't all bad. A fortune hunter would have shown him more attention than Gina had in order to secure his affections. Her caution was appealing. However, that meant she would not be the type of woman who let him measure every bump and curve on a whim.

André flipped through the rest of the notebook, surprised at some of the recent dates. A half-dozen new drawings had appeared in February. Grand-mère must have been watching the shows from New York, London, and Milan. She tended to be inspired by the absurd designs that lacked practicality for any normally shaped woman. As usual, she'd picked out the best of the trends and added the Elinore flare.

What if …? Ideas flowed into his brain.

André's phone had no service. He turned to a page in the back of the book, pulled out a pen, and began sketching and taking notes, then forming a sketch. He filled another page and another until long shadows crossed his page, the sun having sunk behind the tree line. He gathered his things and jogged down the path to his car.

About five minutes into his drive back to Paris, his phone pinged a couple dozen times. Obviously he'd reentered the realm of technology. André guided the car to the side of the road and checked for any critical messages. Neither Gina nor Grand-mère had texted or called. There were a couple more from his father and a few from his cousin, both urging him to give different answers as to his position in the company.

André found the number for Grand-mère's landline.

"Mon petit! You never call!"

Usually he texted Marie or got her to put him on a video call. "Then you know this must be serious. Have you shown any of the designs in your sketchbook to Père or my cousin?"

"Why should I? Arabelle tells me I am an old lady, out of touch with the fashion world. I could produce designs like Arabelle. All I'd have to do is wrap a woman in cellophane and tie a leopard skin bow over her derriere. How can a woman feel powerful in that?"

"Grand-mère, if I accept the position of president, will you allow me the honor of producing these?"

"But of course. You think I would share them with anyone else?"

André didn't have an answer. "Arabelle will not be thrilled if I take over. She will threaten to leave."

Grand-mère snorted a very unrefined sound. "She does every fall. Perhaps it is about time she did."

"I'll call you tomorrow after the negotiations are over."

"When will you see Gina again?"

"Tuesday."

"She is only here for two weeks. You shouldn't waste a day."

"*Bonne nuit*, Grand-mère." The call disconnected.

André texted Gina. **How is the bus tour?**

— Pleasant. Other than the noisy Americans ;)

Any headaches?

— None. Thanks for asking. And how are you?

I took a drive to one of my favorite spots in the wilderness preserve outside Paris. It was nice to be away, only now I have to drive back. May I call you tomorrow?

The dashboard clock ticked, and a car sped by.

—That would be nice.

Bonne nuit.

—Drive safe.

—Thank you for the crêpes.

Anytime.

When no further texts came, André put his phone away and started the car back up, plans for the future swirling through his head.

The tour bus turned down another street, and Gina marked it on her map. Through her headphones, a British female voice discussed the park they were passing and where the next stop would be.

"On your left is the embassy of the Russian Federation." The building had all the charm one would expect from a 1950s cold-war structure, meaning it resembled a prison more than any other building in the area. André had mentioned the embassy yesterday when he'd talked about the location of his grandmother's house. Gina studied her map. The thank-you cards she'd written last night were tucked inside her purse. There should be a mailbox she could drop them in, saving her the embarrassment of asking André for his grandmother's address.

The bus stopped a few blocks down at Musée Marmottan Monet, which she intended to visit next Tuesday. Gina exited the bus and walked back to Elinore's street. She found the building but couldn't get past the gate without a code or being let in by a resident. Not knowing the number of the apartment, Gina returned to the street. The building's exterior lacked the exquisite detail of the interior. She raised her phone and took a photo.

"Mademoiselle! Mademoiselle Gina!" Marie stood in the doorway waving. *"Venez ici."*

Gina did as the woman bid and hurried up the walk.

"Madame saw you from the window. Are you lost?" The housekeeper's heavily accented English sounded musical.

"Non." Gina held up two envelopes. "I only wanted to deliver these cards."

Marie took the offered cards and turned them over in her hands. She held up the one addressed to her. *"Pour moi?"*

Not wanting to state the obvious, Gina nodded.

"Come in. Madame insists I ask. We had her favorite macarons delivered this morning. You will help us eat them?"

"If you insist." Gina followed Marie all the way to the parlor, where the housekeeper handed Elinore her card.

"Welcome. Do sit. I thought I was dreaming when I saw you walk past my window."

Gina smoothed her jean skirt, feeling much too casual to be sitting in the opulent room. "I realized the Musée Marmottan Monet was near your home and wanted to deliver the cards so I didn't have to bother André for your address."

"My grandson would not have considered it a bother." Elinore opened the envelope. "Did you draw this?"

The pen-sketched cupid figure hid behind a banner with the word *merci* scrawled above it. Embarrassment over her inadequate skills flooded her. "Yes?"

"You are not sure? One should always be proud to claim their art. This is good. He looks just like the one I call Gaston." She pointed to one of the carved cupids near the far corner. "His empty bow points to a spot behind that column. I have often wondered how many couples he has caught there over the centuries and induced them to steal a kiss."

"You have pondered them?"

"What else is an old lady to do? Watch television? No. I prefer to use my imagination."

Marie appeared with a tray of brightly colored cookies and turned to leave.

"Sit and eat with us, or I shall be forced to find my cane and shake it at you. Gina is a friend and, as an American, is hardly likely to think you are out of place, n'est-ce pas?"

Gina smiled. "Of course. If only two of us eat all these beautiful macarons, we may become sick, and then I would forever remember my first French macaron with sadness."

The retired housekeeper accepted the invitation. Gina enjoyed the cookies as both Elinore and Marie detailed the names and their thoughts about the many carved cupids.

"I have always felt sorry for Hugo." Elinore indicated a cupid not too far from the naughty ones. "His bow is hanging down. I think he missed the target and the naughty ones, Cupid and Psyche, have been laughing at him forever."

"Perhaps Hugo is the one who shot them." Gina wiped her fingers on the linen napkin.

"That makes sense. Marie, why didn't we think of that?"

Marie shook her head, her mouth full of cookies.

"So, what do you have planned for the rest of your stay in Paris?" asked Elinore.

Gina pulled out her journal. "Tomorrow is Notre-Dame and Île de la Cité. I want to climb to the top, but the website won't allow me to choose a tour time for that until the morning. Then, in the afternoon, I am going with my friends Nick and Zoe Gooding to Galli-Batiste, where André has arranged a tour and an appointment for a fitting. Zoe's husband promised her a Galli-Batiste gown. She is very excited."

"And what about you? Are you excited?"

Marie cleared the tray and didn't return.

Gina chose her words carefully. She'd checked online, and even one of the $300 scarves was well beyond her budget. The T-shirt with the Galli-Batiste logo was half that, but most of the things she liked were in the four-digit price range. "I can't wait to see everything."

"Sadly, our clothes are out of most people's price range. Even I have problems with the exclusivity. It was not always that way. When I first started Galli, my goal was to create things every woman would feel beautiful in. Over the years, the company has lost its vision, and they keep forgetting to invite me to the board meetings ...but I digress. You can't visit Galli-Batiste without getting something. Would you be offended if I offer you any scarf of your choice? André will show you which ones are my designs. They still sell two or three of them and call them 'classic' instead of 'antiquated.'"

"Oh, that is too much."

"Nonsense. Anyone kind enough to deliver hand-drawn thank-you notes can be gracious enough to accept a gift."

"Then I would be delighted."

"May I see your book? I would love to see your drawings close up." Elinore held out her hand.

"They are more like doodles." Gina handed over her bullet journal.

Elinore placed a set of spectacles on her nose. "I think it is delightful. You added these crêpes and cupid last night?" She didn't wait for an answer. "If you skip the catacombs, you can come to luncheon next Sunday and show me your new scarf. At least my bones are not musty and sorted by size."

The ticket she'd purchased was for Sunday afternoon. Maybe they would let her exchange it. "I couldn't possibly turn down another chance to see you."

"*Très bien.* Do you mind if I invite André?"

Gina tried to stop the warmth that flooded her cheeks. "Of course not."

Elinore nodded. "*Merveilleux!* I will get André to text you the time." She looked at the clock. "It is probably time for you to continue your adventures. Permit an old lady one question before you go."

Don't ask about André!

"Are the curls in your hair natural?"

Gina tugged on one lock over her eye, straining it until it touched her chin. "Unfortunately, yes. I've tried straightening them a time or two, but it is not worth it." She let the curl bounce back in place. Inwardly, she sighed in relief. Such an easy question. "When I was little, Mother put it in ponytails and I resembled a poodle. I have the most embarrassing second-grade photo ever."

"It is gorgeous. You are a very lucky woman. Now, if you will excuse me. Marie will come in and insist I take a nap. I oblige her so she will keep ordering macarons." She held out her arms. Gina gave her a hug and kissed her the French way, on each cheek.

On the bus-stop bench, Gina flipped to her bucket-list page and traced the pink circle doodle. One quick kiss wouldn't mean she was having a vacation fling, would it?

André sat across from his father in the soft chairs in one corner of the president's office. Mathieu Batiste sipped his celebratory glass of champagne. "If your uncle was still alive, he would start a lawsuit over this. Your step-cousin still may. But this is the right direction for the company. The method of restructuring should satisfy the entire board. I guess your American MBA was worth every penny."

André took another sip of his Perrier. "How much did you keep designing after you became president?"

"Not much. When your mother died, I lost my muse. I got stuck in the eighties. When you first started here, I thought you would take the place of the head designer. Then Arabelle and Justine tried to take it all from you. In the end, they did that night, n'est-ce pas? Although you hadn't designed for almost five years, the night Justine died is when you gave up."

"I didn't give up. I charted a new course."

"Keep telling yourself that if it helps. Yes, you took the reins of North America and Asia and all nonfashion related entities and made them blossom. I still can't believe we are getting a store back in New York. When it closed in 2010, I thought we would never get a store back there."

"I have an idea for the opening of the store I'd like to run past you." André took Grand-mère's sketchbook from his bag and slid it across the short table. "Grand-mère is still designing. I would like to debut a more affordable clothing line fitting with her original vision when she started her clothing line. Every piece would be under one hundred euros."

"Even this one?"

"Non, she wants me to construct it for her birthday celebration."

"Is she still planning on wearing the dress Pierre designed for her fiftieth birthday? Arabelle stomped around for three days after Grand-mère refused to wear her design."

"Grand-mère didn't design this for herself."

"One of the new models, Terese, would show this off divinely. But your grand-mère is slipping. The proportions are off. I can give it to—"

André reached for the sketchbook. "Grand-mère didn't design it for a model, and she asked me to construct it. I wasn't thinking about that when I showed you the book. It is best if you forget you ever saw it."

"My lips will remain sealed. However, I should have the rest of the book copied so your cousin can have someone start on the new collection."

André put the book back in his bag. "I need to get Grand-mère's approval first. And I would like to wait until the board approves everything else we discussed today. The new designs are part of the deal. One word about them and we are both gone." André debated the ethics of blackmailing his father with the designs as Père wasn't terribly good with secrets.

"So, I can't talk to anyone about your idea? Even Arabelle?"

"Especially not Arabelle." Grand-mère would have a fit if she learned of the plan.

"You didn't let me see the designs in the back of the book. May I see them?"

He hoped his father hadn't realized they were there. "Sorry, Père, those aren't ready for the world to see."

"Not even president yet and already keeping secrets." Mathieu raised his glass. "Good for you, good for you."

The workroom adjoining André's office smelled of fabric dye. A fine coat of dust covered the table. Both signs that in his absence, no one had figured out how to get past his thumbprint pad. André found a cloth to wipe the tables clean. Asking for a custodian would raise eyebrows. Footsteps in the outer office reminded André he needed to activate the motion detector. He met Arabelle at the door to his workroom.

"So, did you and Mathieu reach an understanding?"

"Mathieu will present it to the board Thursday afternoon."

"You know I won't tell."

"Neither will I."

"So, what were you doing in your workroom?"

"Just checking in."

Arabelle narrowed her eyes. "Just thought you would like to know there is a pile of your junk in storeroom B. I need it out of there by the end of the week." She spun and left the room.

André grabbed a set of keys out of his desk. The storeroom was mostly empty. Only the stack of boxes he'd sent himself over the past three years sat in the corner. Four trips later, the entire pile covered his work table. André sorted through it until he found a package from a Chinese silk manufacturer. The color was exactly what he remembered. He called Marie on a video chat.

She was wiping her eyes when she answered.

"Are you all right? Is Grand-mère?"

"Non, all is well. I was just reading the card your girl brought over." Marie showed him a card with an illustration of a strawberry holding a sign saying "Merci." "I can't remember the last time someone wrote a thank-you card other than the ones my daughters force my grandchildren to write each Christmas. She even wrote it in French, although her grammar *est très mauvais.*"

Bad grammar could be fixed. "Gina dropped off a thank-you card at the apartment?"

"Isn't her strawberry the cutest? Then she drew a plate of crêpes and labeled it '*Les meilleures crêpes de Paris.*'" Marie patted her eyes again. "The best crêpes in Paris. Can you believe it?"

"Of course. I grew up eating them."

"But you never sent me a note." She wiped her eyes again. "Oh, I was going to call and invite you to lunch on Sunday. Then you need to text Gina the time of the lunch. And if you are a smart boy, you will also offer to bring her here rather than send her on the metro."

"How did this come about?"

"Well, tomorrow when Gina takes the tour, your grand-mère told her to choose a scarf as her gift. Madame also received a card, but hers has a cupid on it, and she is deeply touched. She said you should not let this tourist go back to the States. And I agree. I like Gina very much."

"So, the lunch invite is so you two can play matchmaker."

"*Mais bien sûr.* What else should two lonely old women do but make sure their favorite man finds love? And with only two weeks, we must act fast so she never wants to go home. We are hoping the cupids will help us."

Too bad their line of thinking was so close to his own. Last night he'd found 5,834 reasons why a relationship wouldn't work. Although it was slightly fewer in miles than kilometers, only 3,625 reasons. If he was returning to continue as the head of North American operations, the list of reasons not to date her shrunk considerably. "The reason I called was to get Grand-mère's opinion on some fabric. Is she around?"

Marie carried the phone into the parlor, aiming the phone camera at the ceiling. "Little cupids, here he is. Shoot your arrows." From the movement of the video, André figured she was trying to let them all see him.

"André, did Marie tell you about our visitor? Although I don't think she intended to visit. She is delightful!" Grand-mère's face filled the screen.

"After speaking with Marie, I may consider wearing chain mail on Sunday."

"Please don't. It stinks to high heaven. We did a show once in '64 and dressed the men as knights in shining armor. I will never forget the smell."

Not wanting a lecture on medieval history, he turned to the subject of the dress. "Last fall when I was in China, I visited a small silk-manufacturing facility. They do small batches of dye, so they are perfect for our one-of-a-kind gowns. I found this and fell in love with it." André attempted to catch the fabric in the best light possible. "The weight and texture are perfect for the style, and the color will complement her skin tone."

"What would you call that color?"

"Midnight China blue. I've never seen quite this shade, but China blue appears to be the base."

"I wish I could see it better." Grand-mère held the phone so close André could see the flecks in her eyes. "Will it go with the lace I chose?"

"I have some up here. I have yet to go through the fabric room." André draped a section of Chantilly lace over the fabric.

"Do you have any black lace?"

André searched and found some black lace. "Sorry this isn't Chantilly, but the color is right."

"Much better. If you don't have any black in the storage room, I have some here. At one point, I had a romantic notion of making myself something black to wear when I became a widow, but Henri got wind of my idea and told me I was not to dress like an old Greek widow until I lived to be 110. I don't think I'll care at that age."

André checked the time. "I'll be by in the morning. I have a general idea of Gina's size and want to start on the pattern tonight."

Marie muttered in the background. "You could go hold her in your arms. Then you'd have a better idea."

"I also wouldn't have time to start on the dress."

Marie turned the phone around so André could see her face. "Youth is wasted on the wrong people."

"*Bon nuit, mesdamess!*" André ended the call before they could give him any more ideas. Gina invaded too many of his thoughts without their help.

The travel site had neglected to describe how steep the four hundred or so steps to the top of Notre-Dame were. One tourist mom must have underestimated the climb and collapsed in a heap on the roof area connecting the north and south towers. Gina hoped the woman's teenage sons would help her back down. But, as the American mother had commented, "The gargoyles and view were worth every step."

The inside of the cathedral was everything she expected and more. Gina could have spent more than an hour studying the paintings, carvings, and stained glass, but the schedule wouldn't allow for that if she was to meet Zoe for lunch before their tour.

It may be the romance of Paris affecting her, but Gina declared the metro to be cleaner than the New York City subway. The people were mostly the same, checking phones and schedules, the tourists huddling around maps. Gina found Nick and Zoe on the opposite corner from where she expected them to be.

Zoe pulled her into a hug. "Isn't Paris amazing? Have you been to the Eiffel Tower yet? We found the kissing spot April told us about. I have the cutest photos."

Over Zoe's shoulder, Nick winked and grinned. It took the entire lunch for Zoe to recount their adventures. "And now a tour and private fitting at Galli-Batiste!"

The best thing about Zoe monopolizing the conversation was that Gina didn't have to talk about her weekend or how she came to meet Elinore Galli. And she didn't need to say André's name. Last night in their video chat, her sister had teased her until Gina had blushed as red as a fire hydrant. The most annoying part of video chats was seeing herself talk.

André waited for them inside the doors of Galli-Batiste. He introduced them to several people, including two women he called stylists. "Before we begin, Nichole and Salome will take you back into the dressing rooms and measure you for your fittings. Nick provided his measurements from his New York tailor. So we will wait for you." His smile melted the cold reserve Gina had built up since Sunday.

Zoe took her arm and marched her into the dressing-room area. "No need to be embarrassed. They are usually fast."

If only that were the cause of her blushes. How could they be explained away when she blushed over the sewing machines and notions later in the tour? The measurement portion ended quickly, considering they'd measured everything from her wrist to her neck length. Nichole even asked her to step onto some kind of foam, making an impression of her foot.

"Oh, I've never done that before. It's like slimy memory foam." Zoe put her own shoes back on.

Gina felt bad for the stylists. Surely they realized there was zero chance she would make a purchase. They rejoined the men, who were discussing real estate taxes in the two countries. "Are we ready, then?" André looked at his phone. "*Je regrette*, but I will need to leave you for part of the tour. My cousin Arabelle Benoit-Galli will show you through. I'll catch up in a moment."

Relief and disappointment warred in Gina as she followed Nick and Zoe through the doors marked "Employees Only." Arabelle spoke quickly, peppering her speech with French phrases. When Zoe asked a question, Arabelle merely shrugged and walked on. How could this rude woman be Elinore's granddaughter?

"Pardon, I saw the interview you did last February on the BBC archive. You mentioned"—Rats, no questions came to mind. Gina only wanted to point out to Arabelle she knew she spoke flawless English—"how you designed your first clothing at age three. What did you design?"

"*Une robe.* A very plain sack dress for my doll." Arabelle's English had improved immensely. André met them at the next room, making the next few minutes more bearable.

"Thank you, Arabelle. Sorry to intrude on your time." He waited for her to leave before continuing. "Your tour proceeded rather quickly. Were there any questions you wanted to ask?"

Zoe asked a question about buttons she'd originally asked Arabelle. Gina looked around the workroom while he answered.

"This is a preconstruction room, where we make a model of the custom dress or suit. This is an especially important step. The prototype is fitted to the client, and the final dress is made from the model. May I show you how we do this? Zoe, would you like to volunteer?"

"No, I think it is Gina's turn." Zoe pushed Gina forward.

André picked up a dress made of white cotton from the table. He held it up to Gina, then picked out a different one. "If you will change into this behind the screen, please. Wear the shirt underneath." André handed her a form-fitting black T-shirt that would cover her to midthigh. "Zoe, if you will help her put this model dress on over the shirt, please."

Gina took the clothing from André, keeping her fingers from touching his.

"You are blushing again. Why are you worried? You will be modest, even if the model dress is lacking." Zoe helped her slip into the dress. If she had been trying on something at her favorite store at home, Gina would have put it into her consider-buying-this pile as the fit was much closer than she expected. She gathered the long skirt and followed Zoe back into the room.

André and Nick waited at the other end, where a round platform stood. André extended his hand. The expected tingle of electricity traveled up her arm at his touch.

"How high of heels do you normally wear with an evening dress?"

Gina spread her thumb and index finger to the height of her favorite heels. André touched her thumb and finger with his own. "Nine centimeters. Do you know your shoe size?"

"Not European. I am a six and a half to seven US." André opened a cupboard filled with shoes and picked out a pair. He knelt next to the platform. "Your foot, mademoiselle?"

Gina extended her foot, still in its sensible walking shoe. André slipped it off, and then her sock. The electricity and coolness of his hand on her foot made her giggle.

"Ah, so you are of the variety with ticklish feet. According to Grand-mère, Queen Antonetta was too, so much so they had the most difficult time creating her shoes for the royal wedding." He worked quickly as he spoke.

When he stood, they were eye to eye. Gina moved her gaze to the mirror behind him, trying not to double-check to see whether his eyes did indeed have green flecks.

"This dress fit is not perfect. If we are making a dress worth twenty thousand euros, then perfect is the only acceptable fit. So we do a bit of this and that." André pulled a seam here and added a pin there.

Gina resisted the urge to shiver as his hands skimmed over the dress.

"I didn't realize you were a fashion designer as well." Nick's voice broke the silence.

"How could I not be? Ma mère gave me my first sketchbook before my second birthday. By age five, I could tell a fine silk from a cheap satin. Until five years ago, I was an active part of the design team." André used a pen to make several marks on the cotton dress. "And there you have it—ready to be used as a pattern for a fine gown."

Gina took his hand and stepped down. She looked in the mirror. "I can't believe the difference a few pins can make. Too bad this isn't a real gown. It is fit for a princess."

Zoe joined her. "Or Cinderella's fairy godmother's wand."

"Hang the model dress over the screen. Be careful with the pins."

Zoe got the zipper halfway down. "It's stuck." She tugged at it a couple more times. "André, we have a problem with the zipper."

André came around the screen. "Do not look so worried. Hold the dress in the front. The zipper won't go lower than the T-shirt."

Gina bit her lip and looked at the ceiling as André's hands worked to open the zipper. The intimacy of having him practically undress her caused her cheeks to burn.

"It will be easiest if you step out of the dress." André disappeared around the screen, and Gina put her clothes on. André leaned against the worktable, waiting. Nick and Zoe were nowhere to be seen. Gina offered the black T-shirt to André.

"The shirt is yours to keep. If we were doing a real gown, we would keep the shirt and shoes in a special bag for you to use at every fitting. Eventually, you would bring your own shoes or the shoes one of our designers created for you."

Gina folded the shirt and stuffed it in her bag.

"My sincere apologies if I embarrassed you."

Gina shook her head. "It is fine. Where are the Goodings?"

"Her stylist was ready, which is the end of the tour, so I told them to go ahead."

"Is something wrong?" André ran his fingers down the side of her face and lifted her chin with one finger.

Everything! Your eyes are greener than I thought they were. I am alone with you, and I made a list of ten reasons why this is a bad idea. Her breath hitched as André's face moved closer. Gina closed her eyes. To kiss or not to kiss? Head and heart warred over the answer.

His breath brushed her skin.

Gina turned her head away and stepped back.

Disappointment surged through André when his lips met air. Never in the history of Paris had a man been more confused. Surely he hadn't forgotten all the signs and signals—the blushes, coy glances, the racing pulse—during his hiatus from the dating world.

Gina stood a couple feet away from him, her hand over her mouth, her eyes wide, her body shaking. "I'm sorry!" She dashed for the doorway only to be tripped by the nine-centimeter heels she'd neglected to take off. She lay on the floor for a second.

The inner hero was all for scooping her up and carrying her over to the platform and helping her change her shoes, but common sense won out, and he cautiously offered a hand. "Hurt?"

Gina stood on wobbly feet. "Just my pride. That is a good antitheft device you have in the shoes." Tears leaked from the corners of her eyes, diminishing the value of her brave smile. Gina limped over to the platform and sat on the edge.

André followed, grabbing a box of imported American facial tissues on the way. He doubted she would appreciate them, but the soft, lotioned tissues were one of the little things he had learned to enjoy while living in the States. He set the box between them and sat next to her. "I'm sorry. I should have asked permission—"

Gina took a tissue and blew her nose before answering. "No, it's not that. I would have said yes and still turned away. For two crazy days, I thought ...I thought I could do this, but I shouldn't. When I felt you so near, I wanted—" Her words sped up as her hands waved between them. "I'm not a sixteen-year-old who thinks a vacation romance can be as amazing as some sappy novel. The only way the relationship ends is with wounded hearts and memories of kissing a hot Frenchman."

Hot? Wrong takeaway. "You pulled back because you didn't want us to be a 'fling'? I think that is the right word."

"Fling covers it. At my age, I—"

"*Ma chérie*, you are not old, but I think I understand. You may not believe me, but I don't go kissing every tourist I meet." The few dates he'd gone on since Justine's death had ended with no more than a kiss on the cheek. Under normal circumstances, he would not have moved so quickly for a kiss, but he had only ten days to give her a reason to start a long-distance relationship that could grow into something else.

"I am sorry I didn't realize sooner. I feel like I led you on." Gina handed him the heels.

André pointed to her left cheek. "You have a smear—"

Gina rubbed near the spot but missed. André shook his head. "May I?"

She held out her tissue.

He took a fresh one. "*Je suis désolé de ne pas avoir voulu te faire pleure.* There you go—as good as new. Ready to go try on some clothes?"

Her brow furrowed at his apology in French. "I'm not sure I should. We both know I will not purchase anything. I don't want to waste the valuable time the staff could be serving paying customers."

"Sometimes, ma chérie, the memory is the most important part of the moment. Unlike our clothes, the memory will never go out of style."

"Well …"

André stood. "Before you say no, remember, Grand-mère wants you to choose a scarf."

Gina stood and took three tentative steps forward. "Like I said, only my pride was injured."

André escorted her out of the room and wished only his pride hurt.

12

The blue-and-gold silk scarf outshone everything in her wardrobe. It didn't go with the sundress she planned on wearing on Sunday. Too bad she couldn't afford the blue Godot skirt and blouse Nichole had found for her to try on. She'd twirled twice in the dressing-room mirror before emerging to show Zoe and everyone else. Appreciation had shown in André's eyes—not that she had looked. That would be stupid after falling on her face and running out on his kiss.

Gina suppressed the voice telling her she would regret her choice for the rest of her life. When Zoe had asked questions, Gina only told her about the fall.

Turning her attention back to her wardrobe, Gina wondered if she could find a button-down shirt at a reasonable price. No use longing for the blouse she'd tried on. According to the Galli-Batiste website, the scarf alone cost roughly the same as an advance-purchase coach ticket from JFK to Charles de Gaulle Airport. Gina added that fact to the list of reasons she'd made the right choice with the kiss. French billionaires didn't have long-term relationships with American peasants.

Her phone pinged.

— Grand-mère wonders if Sunday at thirteen hundred works for lunch. She doesn't know about today, but if you'd rather not come ...

One is fine. Just because we did or didn't or whatever, I wouldn't blow Elinore off, unless you want me to. I feel so honored she would invite me.

— She is excited you will come. I am keeping the scarf you chose a secret. She is annoyed with me. She might uninvite me.

I don't think she will.

—Speaking of invitations . . . I have yours for the party on Monday. I forgot to give it to you.

Do I need to drop by and pick it up?

—I can bring it to your hotel.

With the number of second thoughts she'd entertained about seeing him tonight, it would be a terrible idea. **I don't want to make you go out of your way.**

—Where are you headed tomorrow?

First of two days at the Louvre. I can stop by the store.

—I can't leave the invitation downstairs. There are reporters who would pay thousands.

Oh, I had no idea. *Should I back out? I have nothing to wear*! If the invitation came from André rather than his grandmother, she could graciously bow out. **Can I meet you?**

—I'm leaving work now. Can I come by the hotel?

I'm not ready to see you. I'll be waiting in the lobby.

—See you in fifteen minutes.

Fifteen minutes to get her emotions under control. It would be easier to run a 5k in that time. The twenty-two-minute 5K she ran last year to benefit the crisis center had nearly killed her. That random fact helped lower her heart rate. Unfortunately, there were not enough random facts in her personal knowledge base to lower her heart rate to near zero to combat the effects of André's presence. She took the staircase down three floors to the lobby. A French comedy played on the television. Gina concentrated on following the storyline, surprised at how much

French she actually remembered. So far, every time she'd tried to use her rudimentary language skills to order at a café or bakery, she'd received an answer in English. André always spoke to her in English—other than his apology for making her cry, which sounded better in French.

She pushed the thought out of her mind and focused on the comedy. If the canned laughter was any indication, Gina understood most of the jokes—although, like American sitcoms, they were not nearly as funny as the producers assumed they were.

"I'm impressed you laughed at the pun," André said in French, startling Gina as he walked up behind her.

"I took enough in college to read *Les Mis*. My conversational French is lacking." Gina answered in English. "Nothing like your practically flawless English."

"Practically?"

"The first time we met, your accent was much more pronounced."

"Sometimes that happens around beautiful women. More attractive than a stammer, non?" His accent was the heaviest she'd heard yet.

"Or you are trying to flirt?"

"Mais oui, American women swoon at the sound."

Gina rolled her eyes.

André held out an envelope. "Your golden ticket. You will need the invitation to enter the Musée Rodin, even if you allow me to be your escort."

"You don't have a plus-one already?"

"Non, I was planning on being at Grand-mère's side, but she asked my father to escort her."

"A recent development?"

"Sunday afternoon."

Part of Elinore's not-so-subtle matchmaking campaign, no doubt. "If you are asking as my friend, I am more than happy to go with you."

"I'll text you the time I'll pick you up."

"Thanks, André." Gina stood, hoping he would take the hint and leave before her resolution dissolved.

"As your friend, you will still text me if you get into a situation where you need help?"

"Sure." Not that it would happen. Saturday's headache was nothing more than a lack of sleep. And she hadn't had a regular headache since before arriving at JFK.

He scowled for a moment. "I need to go. Grand-mère wanted to speak about a project."

Gina held up the envelope. "Thank you for bringing this by. Have a good night."

Only after he left did she realize he hadn't kissed her on the cheek at his greeting.

Carrying a large package under his arm, André let himself into Grand-mère's apartment. The light was on in the workroom, where Grand-mère dozed in a chair in the corner. André set the package on the table.

"You're late."

"Sorry, I ran an errand on my way."

"Let me see." Elinore stood and waved at the box.

André lifted the lid and took out the muslin model dress he'd fitted on Gina as well as the silk wrapped in a sheet of protective muslin.

Elinore rubbed a corner of the silk between her fingers. "Exquisite. Do you have enough for the dress?"

"I purchased six meters."

"More than enough. Do you have my sketchbook?"

André pulled the book out. "I spoke to Père about doing a line based on your clothing. I would like the bulk of the line to be something affordable to the middle class and perhaps even marketed by a midlevel chain store. Then I bribed him to keep his mouth shut."

"I like that very much. It bothers me that over the years our store has become so exclusive only the wealthiest can shop there. Which reminds me—which scarf did Gina choose?"

"I told you that you can see it on Sunday, but she did choose one of your classic designs without any prompting."

"I knew mademoiselle had excellent taste. Now, tell me why there is sadness in your voice when you speak of her." Elinore pulled up a low-backed stool and sat at the worktable.

André put the silk away and spread out the model dress. "I was stupid. I thought if I kissed her she would understand how much she intrigues me. I never met a woman who pulls at my heart so much."

"You moved too fast, André." Elinore nodded. "Any single person in their thirties has experienced a bruised and battered heart. Her Prince Charming may have turned out to be a villain, or she kissed one-to-many frogs to believe in happily ever after. Not everyone's story is in their Wikipedia profile, and even then, the truth is far different."

"You have read my page?"

"Of course. They connect it to mine, which is far more accurate."

"Do you mind if I finish the construction here? Arabelle has been nosing about. I caught her in my office again."

Elinore waved at the table and the dress forms in the corner. "She hasn't seen my book, has she?"

"No, I have kept your sketches on my person or locked away in my safe." André chose a dress form and adjusted it to the measurements Nichole had taken on Gina.

"While you lay out the pattern, you can tell me how you got Gina's measurements."

"Better than that, I got her to try this on." André held up the model dress and launched into the story of his afternoon. By the time he finished, he had the muslin model dress deconstructed.

Elinore opened her book to the page where she'd designed

the dress and compared the book to the pattern in front of her. "Did you add a hidden pocket?"

"Yes. I discovered most American women prefer to be near their phones. And Gina only has a bulky cross-shoulder purse with her."

"If you have the fabric, make her a matching clutch, or one of the black ones will do, as long as it is not beaded. If she holds a beaded bag under her arm, it will rip the lace." Elinore flipped through the rest of the pages. As she closed the book, André breathed a sigh of relief. Then she opened the book to the last pages. "What is this? You drew in my book?"

"*Je regrette*. The ideas came, and your sketchbook was all I had with me."

"This one—a wedding dress, n'est-ce pas? On a curly haired model ..."

André swallowed but didn't answer the obvious.

"She uncurled one of her bangs for me. It reached past her chin. I suspect she would want an updo on her wedding day. You should change the veil. I knew you hadn't lost your touch." Elinore extended a hand for him to help her down from her stool. "It's past my bedtime. Don't stay up too late. I ruined more gowns that way. That is how narrower skirts came into fashion one year."

André kissed Grand-mère. "I was not going to cut the silk tonight."

Elinore patted his cheek. "Do not worry, mon trésor. She likes you. All is not lost."

André let himself out. Driving home, he passed one of the lesser-known cathedrals, Eglise la Trinité, with its statue of St. Jude, the patron saint of lost causes, the one he needed now.

13

If she had opened the invitation last night when André stood in the lobby, she could have asked. Gina typed the words into her phone again. This translator app had to be wrong, just like the other two. Gina ran through the few French expletives she knew, but they didn't help. *Soirée habillée* still translated to something akin to a black-tie event. Even at home, she didn't own an evening gown appropriate for an event hosted for one of the most famous fashion designers in the world. Years ago, she'd read an autobiographical account of an actress who'd spent a summer in Paris. One afternoon, the actress was invited as a plus-one to a formal party. That morning she purchased a long black bohemian-style skirt. The actress wore the skirt as a halter dress and no one had seemed to care. Given the things Gina had seen in fashion-week videos, perhaps she could find something at a secondhand shop and find a way to make it work. Or Zoe ...they were close in size.

Hey, did you bring a black dress?

— Why? André?

Not André but his family.

— The hundredth birthday?

How do you know?

— It is all over the papers.

Gina picked up the invitation. No wonder the calligraphy looked hand-lettered and not computer generated. Her phone rang.

"I'd have you come for breakfast, but we are leaving for Versailles and Chartres as soon as the driver gets here. We won't be back until Thursday night. Now spill."

"Hello, Zoe, thanks for calling." Gina suppressed a laugh.

"You knew it was me. How did you get a ticket to the event? André apologized to Nick for not realizing he would be in the country sooner and said there were no invitations left."

"André didn't invite me. Elinore did."

There was dead air on the other end of the line.

"Zoe?"

"I'm here. You've been holding out on me. You met Elinore Galli and didn't tell me?"

"You are here as a newlywed. It just hasn't come up."

"What is going on with André—and don't tell me nothing."

Gina sighed. "There might be some attraction, but I burned my bridge yesterday in the most spectacular manner."

"Oh." Zoe paused but didn't pry. "So, you need a dress? I brought the proverbial little black dress with me. You are welcome to borrow it. Though the dress isn't that little, as it is more of a maxi skirt."

"You're a lifesaver."

"We can get together on Saturday. You're going to Chartres tomorrow?"

"Yes, I purchased my train ticket already."

"Our driver is here. Have a good day!"

Gina smiled at her now-silent phone. Marriage worked well for Zoe. Hopefully the dress would fit. Some place in Paris should sell spandex.

Gina gathered her things and an extra protein bar. Today would be her long day at the Louvre as the museum didn't close until ten o'clock tonight. Gina locked the invitation in the hotel safe, along with the scarf. If only her heart fit in there too.

"Why aren't you in the board meeting?" Arabelle plopped into the chair opposite André's desk.

"Probably for the same reason you aren't."

"They asked you to leave too?"

"Not invited."

"Did you know your grand-mère was here? She almost never attends."

"No, I hadn't seen her today."

Arabelle leaned on his desk. "I don't think you deserve to be president. You have been absent from Paris since the accident. Never came for fashion week."

"Do you have a complaint about my work in Asia and North America?"

"I heard you yesterday talking with an American accent to those people."

"And I heard you pretending not to understand. I assume you missed the memo that the couple you rushed through your tour are Nick and Zoe Gooding, recently wed and of the New York Goodings. And in case you failed to recognize the name, it appears above any of the Galli-Batiste family on the Forbes list of billionaires. The New York store will reside in one of Gooding's buildings. So they are probably the last American billionaires you should try to offend."

Arabelle sat down, her face draining of color. "Neither woman was dressed ..."

"Hardly an excuse not to treat them with respect. They are on vacation and dressed comfortably."

"Is the other woman a billionaire too?"

Not yet. "She is a good friend of Madame Gooding. I am not privy to her bank account, but it does not matter, does it? We don't treat customers that way at Galli-Batiste."

"Oh." Arabelle shifted in the seat. "Well, at least Madame Gooding still ordered. I didn't ruin everything. I don't think the other one could purchase off our seconds rack."

He'd forgotten the bargains found there. If the skirt Gina tried on yesterday …Talking in the hall interrupted his musings.

"Board meeting went quick." Arabelle stood to leave.

His father's secretary stood in the doorway. "Didn't expect to find you together, but it saves me time. The board requests your presence."

Arabelle sauntered down the hallway. André took a moment to straighten his tie.

Except for Grand-mère, everyone stood when Arabelle and André entered. They sat in the two empty seats at the end of the table.

While everyone else took their seats, Mathieu remained standing. "We have known for some time that today would come. I am retiring as president of Galli-Batiste International. Although I will keep my shares and a position on the board, I will no longer be over the day-to-day operations of the company. Thirty years ago, Henri Galli gave my wife the title of president, one which she declined as she desired to see André more often than the job would allow. My wife loved designing—something she claimed she could do as well from the dining room table. I held this position for thirty years, whether I should have or not." He nodded to his secretary. "Please read the vote from this morning."

The secretary stood. "After some spirited debate, it was proposed by Mathieu Batiste and seconded by Elinore Galli that André Henri Batiste be named the new president of Galli-Batiste International effective May 1 of this year. The voting held by secret ballot was unanimous in the affirmative."

Arabelle squeaked, her face turning red. André expected her to stomp out of the room, but she remained and clapped with the others.

Mathieu walked around the table and kissed André on each cheek. "Congratulations, son."

Grand-mère rapped on the table. "Before André gives his words of acceptance, I have a few things I would like to say. First, I expected I would leave the board at least ten years ago, yet I am still here—a fact we will all celebrate on Monday. On the following Wednesday, I will step down as chairman. I believe anyone with three digits in their age column should enjoy their last few days in peace. According to my will, all my shares go to André and his wife. Since he has no wife, they will be held in trust for her for the next ten years, by which time I may take up haunting him, even if I still enjoy life from this side of the grave." Everyone in the room laughed, although some laughs sounded more nervous than others. "My last act as chairman of the board will be to announce the changing of the guard. The media is already speculating. Let them speculate. If anyone in this room so much as whispers the proceedings of today outside this room, remember, I have the power to fire you. Now, André, rush through your acceptance so we can go to lunch."

Again, laughter erupted.

André stood. "I attended my first board meeting in this very room about thirty-five years ago. Not that I remember the occasion, but there is a photo of Grand-père holding me in his seat at the head of the table. I know some will claim I was given this job because of my fortunate birth. But I hope this board at least understands I will continue to give an honest day's work, as Grand-père expected me to, as president of Galli-Batiste International. And, as my first motion, I would like to propose we adjourn for lunch."

Arabelle shot him a venomous look and left. André accepted everyone's congratulations.

Grand-mère pulled him aside and kissed him on each cheek. "Have dinner with me tonight."

Mathieu was last to leave. "It goes without saying, but I'd watch out for Arabelle. She's spent most of the last two years campaigning for this position. I think a couple of the board members voted more against her than they voted for you."

André nodded. Arabelle wasn't the first conniving woman he'd dealt with. Sadly, the friendship they shared as children had died with Justine. André accompanied several of the board members to lunch in the private dining room of an elite restaurant.

One of the board members who'd designed under his mother pulled him aside, laying an arthritic hand on his arm. "I nearly didn't vote for you. I think a man in your position needs to be in a healthy, long-term relationship. But with the alternative being Arabelle …I'll be watching you."

André nodded in agreement. He had the woman and the dress all picked out. He waited until he could text discreetly and sent one text.

I hope you are enjoying the Louvre.

No return text came.

14

$\mathcal{D}$id artists create works about anything other than love? Gina retreated to the apartments of Napoleon III in the Richelieu wing, searching for a reprieve after the sculptures. Not that she would forget *Psyche Revived by Cupid's Kiss* soon. A kiss strong enough to wake Psyche from a never-ending sleep. The thought nagged at Gina, who felt as if she'd sleepwalked most of the morning through the museum. The Richelieu wing was nearly devoid of tourists, and finding a deserted bench near the elevators, Gina searched her museum app, hoping to justify her constant thoughts about a certain new French aquaintance. Relatively few pieces in the collection came up under searches for *love* or *kiss*.

A text from her mother came in.

—**Good morning. Or is it afternoon? Hope all is going well. How is your man?**

Late afternoon. Assume he is fine, but not mine.

—**????**

Gina didn't respond. Instead, she surreptitiously ate a few bites of a protein bar.

She ignored André's text.

When she wasn't feeling like typing something like "I'm an idiot. Can I have a do-over?" she'd text him back.

She wandered through the rooms, looking at furniture and housewares from bygone eras and longing to run her fingers over the wood. How had the craftsmen created such works without electric sanders or laser cutting? The plate made with a three-dimensional snake, fish, and crawdad made her shudder. She wouldn't have been able to eat for a week after seeing food on that.

Two days would not be enough to explore the entire museum. Her plan of exploring all day and ending with *Mona Lisa* near nine when the lines should be shorter would not work. There was too much to take in and too much to see, and most tourists only got a day. Gina entered the glorious sculpture atrium she'd bypassed earlier. Yes, far too much to see. Near the end of her wanderings in the area, she was surprised to find all the exits blocked by guards. She soon learned that the wing was temporarily closed off from the rest of the museum due to an "incident." As the benches in the room were already filled with patrons, Gina found a vacant step and pulled out her journal. A third day at the Louvre meant missing a day or afternoon at other museums. Gina studied the museum app and concluded she best follow her plan to visit the *Mona Lisa*, the painting made famous because someone had stolen it.

—**Mom says you broke up with André! What's up with that?**

Screaming in the middle of the Louvre during a lockdown? Not wise. Guards would swarm, and André would get a call from a French jail. She should have kept her mouth closed during the video call and never mentioned him.

Mom is reading entire novels between the lines of my texts. You can't break up with someone you aren't dating.

— **But he took you to his grandma's.**

He killed two birds with one stone. Feed me and visit family.

— **Stop being so cynical. Not every guy is Bob, Fred, or Jon, or whatever other jerks you've dated.**

I never dated a Bob or a Jon. Fred only managed one date. He still lives with his mother.

—You know what I mean. I've seen his photo . . . if I weren't married. . . Talk later. I haven't seen the Mona Lisa yet.

Gina put her phone in airplane mode, where she could still access the museum information she'd downloaded yet ignore all texts. When the guards opened the door, she followed the other patrons out of the room.

Viewing the European paintings was like watching a team of gymnasts score perfect tens one after another. The time she'd allotted herself here flew by. Gina joined the other tourists for a closer view of the most famous painting in the building. Less than twenty people stood in front of it. The number of people taking selfies annoyed her. The vision in her left eye flickered, and the room dimmed.

No! No! No!

Gina followed the others through the line. When it was her turn to stand in front of the famous painting, she covered her right eye. The halo-and-flash effect added a psychedelic feel to Da Vinci's work. The American family in front of her was discussing a late-night dinner. Gina stayed behind them in hopes of following them to the nearest exit, but she lost them in the crowd. Fortunately, most patrons seemed to be heading out, and she soon found herself in the Pyramid reception area. She'd looked at the map enough today to know she could get to the metro through the mall, which had closed over an hour ago. She wasn't sure if she could safely pass through the area or ride the metro in her current condition.

Pulling out her phone, she closed her right eye and sent a text.

— Headache. Louvre Pyramid reception area. Please advise on best way out.

André read the text and checked the time. If every light in Paris worked in his favor, he could get to the Louvre in fifteen minutes, but the chances of finding a parking space were minimal. At least he had the tiny Citroën tonight. He left Grand-mère's workroom to find Marie and Grand-mère watching a reality fashion show on TV. "Gina has one of her headaches. She's at the Louvre. I'll be back."

Coming! Should be there in fifteen. Sit down and wait.

— Okay, need plan B if you don't make it.

If I am not there, go up the stairs and stay close to the Pyramid.

— Thanks.

St. Jude worked overtime. Thirteen minutes later, André was pulling into a parking space less than two blocks from the Louvre. Raindrops fell as he dashed for the Pyramid entrance, the closest to where Gina was. He called, hoping for enough reception to answer.

"Hello?"

"I am coming to the Pyramid entrance. Can you see to come up the stairs and out, or do I need to come in?"

"I see the stairs to my left—"

The line went dead.

The courtyard in front of the Pyramid hosted a few scattered tourists bright enough to bring umbrellas.

A guard at the entrance stopped André. *"Le musée sera fermée dans cinq minutes. Pas d'entrer."*

Just as he expected—no entry five minutes before closing. André pulled out his wallet. Earlier that day while going through his desk, he'd found his annual pass showing his donation status and had added the card to his wallet in case he had a chance to go with Gina. The guard's eyes widened. André held up his photo ID. "Please, five minutes. My friend is inside, and she is ill."

The guard looked at the door, then back to the pass he held. He handed back the card and held up his hand, his fingers spread out. *"Cinq minutes."*

Halfway down the stairs, he spotted Gina making her way along a wall to the bottom of the stairway. He hurried to intercept her.

"Gina?"

She threw her arms around him, then quickly stepped back. "Sorry, I shouldn't have done that."

"Why not?"

"Cultural differences. I remember learning something about the French not even having a good word for *hug*."

Too bad. He'd definitely let her hug him again. André tucked her right hand in his elbow. "No one else is on the stairs. Can you see the handrail?" She caught the top bar with her left hand before he continued. "I've lived in the US long enough I don't flinch at spontaneous hugs. So if you ever want to try again …"

Gina blushed but didn't answer.

"So, when did this headache start?"

"Just as I got to the *Mona Lisa*. The vision in my mind is more like rock-concert lighting meets Da Vinci. I think he may have liked it that way. How did you get in here?"

"Annual pass with the family's donor status. I think the guard was almost as worried about the consequences of not letting me in." They turned up at the last landing. "There he is now." André nodded to the guard. "Merci."

"*Bonne nuit.*"

A few steps away from the door, Gina stopped and pulled her hand from André's arm to dig through her bag. She handed him a travel umbrella, then checked all the zippers on her purse.

André opened the umbrella.

"I made you run in the rain, didn't I? Thanks for coming to get me. I didn't dare take the metro like this. Although I may have found it …"

André held the umbrella over both of them. "How did you get from the *Mona Lisa* to the entrance hall?"

"Easy. I followed noisy American tourists. I don't understand how I got a migraine today."

"What did your doctor say about them?"

"The usual—stress, eyestrain, and no idea."

Could the stress be because of him? "How long have you been in the Louvre?"

"Since it opened."

"Did you leave for lunch?"

"I had a protein bar. I hid while I ate it."

"And dinner?"

"A second protein bar."

"You realize those things don't count as food. You are in Paris. Cuisine was invented here. I think there should be a line in the tourist guides saying compressed soybean products are not allowed."

"Yes, but there are over thirty thousand works on display, and I only have two days."

"And now you haven't even really seen the *Mona Lisa.*"

"I must get there early next Wednesday so I can see her first. There is something wrong about not seeing her, even if I think she is overhyped."

"May I take you to dinner?"

"I don't want to keep you from what you were doing. Nick and Zoe are spending the night out in Chartres or I would have called them or waited—"

"Gina." He stopped walking and turned to face her. "It wasn't a bother to come find you, neither is taking you to dinner." *Please agree. Give me a second chance. Give us a chance.*

She'd waited a heartbeat too long. "Thanks. I would love to eat with you."

"My car is this way. Unless you prefer McDonald's."

"I may be willing to eat a protein bar to keep looking at works of art, but I draw the line at eating Mc-Food in Paris. But nothing huge. I am perfectly fine with Nutella crêpes." She dropped her hand and covered her eyes one after the other.

"Eyesight coming back?"

"Some." Gina checked the time on her phone. "I guess I could have made it to closing after all and you could have stayed out of the rain."

"I'm not complaining." André stopped next to his little Citroën and opened the door for Gina, keeping the umbrella over her head as she got in. The storm abated, the clean smell of spring rain permeating the Paris street and washing away the everyday grime and smells of the city. It was the promise of a new start, even for the old streets. If only it was as easy to wash yesterday away and find a fresh start with Gina.

Thoughts and feelings she suppressed all day bounced inside Gina like the pinball video game she'd played as a child. Only the ball in this game seemed to be repeatedly hitting her heart and her brain. She had just called one of the wealthiest men in Paris from who knows what at nine thirty at night to come to save her. She wouldn't dare call up any of New York's wealthiest to do the same—other than Nick and Zoe, but that was different. Even more astounding was that he had come. Surely he could have just found a driver or employee to save her. After yesterday's non-kiss, his willingness to help her reinforced the idea that she'd missed an opportunity for a relationship worth taking a risk on.

As André got in, he tossed the umbrella in the back seat. "How hungry are you?"

"Not as much as I should be. Unlike normal migraines, I'm not sick to my stomach, but my body worries I might be."

"I should introduce you to my favorite comfort food, *gratin dauphinois*—potatoes, cream, and cheese under a crunchy topping."

"Sounds delicious." And quick and easy.

As André turned onto the Champs-Élysées, Gina closed her eyes to block out the street lights. A touch on her knee startled her.

"Are you all right?"

No, I'm regretting my life choices. "The street lights are not helpful at the moment."

"Understandable."

The car made a right turn. Gina opened her eyes to find they'd turned onto a narrow street devoid of bright lights. She doubted this was the most direct route to his destination. André turned several more times before parking in a space a few doors down from a restaurant.

Delicious smells peppered with garlic and oregano filled the air. Their table sat against an old brick wall. Gina squinted at her menu.

"Do you mind if I order for you?"

"Thanks, I am still—" She waved her hand in front of her eyes. "Do they serve the *gratin dauphinois*?"

"Of course. Do you prefer water or wine?"

"Water, please. The Perrier."

A server came, and André ordered.

Gina couldn't see his face well in the low lighting. Perhaps if she spoke, her thoughts would calm down. "I wanted to apologize for yesterday. I didn't handle things very well. I mean ...I—" Gina took a deep breath. An awkward teenager would be able to explain it better. "I wish we had more than two weeks—"

His hand covered hers on the table. "I should apologize. I rushed when I should have waited." He ran his thumb over her knuckles, sparks dancing up her arm.

"If we lived in the same place, would yesterday still have happened?" The question wasn't exactly what she meant, but hopefully it was close enough.

"If you mean would I have wanted to kiss you, the answer is yes. Would I have followed through? Probably not yet."

The server interrupted them, and she moved her hand to her lap, where it would be safe from the sensations he was stirring in her. The *gratin dauphinois* surpassed her expectations. Gina ate out of need and to keep words from forming before she contemplated them.

"Have you been in a long-distance relationship before?" asked André.

Mouth full, Gina shrugged. André waited.

"Once in college, I thought I was. He didn't."

"Am I correct in assuming you are more concerned about having a 'fling' than having a relationship with me?"

The water in Gina's mouth threatened to come back out, the minerals and bubbles burning. Heat rose in her cheeks. At last, her swallowing mechanism worked again. "Yes," she squeaked. "I mean, I'm not opposed to getting to know you better. But I've never been a one-night-stand sort of person."

"Neither have I."

Gina took a bite of some meat dish. Flavors she couldn't place reminded her of her grandmother's cooking. "So where does that leave us?"

"Did you know I am purchasing an apartment in Nick's building?"

"The Plaza? I had no idea." That would make a long-distance relationship easier.

"What I am trying to say is we have more options than most if we continue exploring us."

"So we could stop trying to squish things into ten more days?"

André paused before answering. "I want to get to know all of you, not just a condensed version."

"I would like that." Gina finished the last bite on her plate.

André yawned as he cut the last piece of silk. The two hours he'd spent with Gina had cost him in sleep. He would not complete the dress by Sunday unless he worked tonight.

After comparing schedules, they decided the next time they could meet was Friday afternoon, for the Eiffel Tower. At least that would give him all of Thursday evening to work. Another yawn overtook him, and he put his scissors away. Anything he did from this point on would need to be redone. At seventy euros a meter, a wrong cut could be devastating. He covered the work-table with a sheet, turned out lights, and closed the workroom.

Dim light illuminated the hallway around the kitchen door. Grand-mère sat at the table, stirring up a cup of chocolate. "Finished for tonight?"

"I'm not as far as I want to be, but I'll have the dress finished by Sunday morning."

"The smile is back in your eyes. Anything to do with Gina?"

André took a mug down and filled it with chocolate. "We had one of those functional and unromantic discussions over dinner. We decided to see where things might go. I told her I was getting a pied-à-terre in New York, but I couldn't tell her I wouldn't be there as much as I planned on. If things work out, I'll collect enough miles to send a dozen terminally ill children to Florida."

"You need to tell her about Justine's death. With Arabelle so upset about your new position, she might try to use her version of her step-father's death as a wedge between you and everyone else."

"Why would she do that? The past must be as painful for her."

"She didn't leave the country for three years."

"Arabelle also didn't like her stepfather as much as she did his name. I don't think they talked for months before he died."

"But she thinks she deserves everything you have. Her name is still Batiste."

André swallowed the cold chocolate. "What should I do about her?"

"I can't answer that, she will never be happy working for you, I don't believe she has the spine to go off on her own just yet. But when she does, she will take every designer loyal to her with her."

Not acquainted enough with half the designers, he had no idea who that might be. "That may not be entirely bad."

"Maybe not. And I know you can lead Galli-Batiste through it, or I would not have put my vote behind you." She drained her cup. "However, I'd rather have you lose Galli-Batiste than the chance at lasting happiness. Henri and I were happy, and your mother and father had the same thing. You and Justine didn't. Life is nothing without love. Henri and I lived through difficult days where we didn't know if there would be a next meal or if we'd trusted the wrong person. The one thing I knew each night as Henri wrapped his arms around me was that we were better together, whether facing Hitler's soldiers or the expectations of the press over my dress for the First Lady of the United States. I so desperately wish the same for you, and I want to live long enough to see it."

A lump formed in André's throat. "I wish you to be here too. But like you told me when ma mère died, I know you'll be watching from above."

"Well, I am not there yet." Grand-mère pushed herself back from the table.

"I can't make you any promises, but the more I talk with her, the more I wish to talk to her. Does that make any sense?"

"That is how it should be when one is in love." Grand-mère set her cup in the sink. "Bonne nuit, mon trésor."

The clock in the parlor struck one. André locked the door behind him and hoped the day would speed by.

16

—How was Chartres?

Gina smiled at André's text as she kicked her shoes off.

Just like I imagined it, only better. The architecture of the cathedral—amazing. *And lonely.* In the past decade, Gina often traveled alone, mostly to business meetings, but today, for the first time, she'd felt the need to share her discoveries. The flower she didn't know the name of. The kitschy souvenir so silly she bought one for her sister. The windows in the cathedral.

—**Any headaches?**

No, I ate real food. Soup and bread. And I didn't feel as stressed.

—**Good. I wish I could see you tonight.**

Me too. I walked my feet off—23,456 steps. I think an early night will be good for me. How was your day?

Rubbing the soles of her feet, Gina wished they'd equipped the room with a tub just so she could soak them.

— **Work was interesting. I am finishing up some things now. I don't want to be late tomorrow afternoon.**

I'll wait for you if you are. Her heart took over for her fingers before she could hit the Delete key.

— **If you must, go up at your assigned time. I'll be there.**

Did you get a ticket, then? All day she thought of things to talk about, and now she couldn't come up with a thing to say.

— **Yes. I wouldn't miss it.**

Her heart hit a few staccato beats. **How many billions of times have you been up there?**

—**Probably as many times as you have been to the top of the Empire State Building.**

Twice?

— **At least five.**

Won't you be bored?

— **Seeing it with you will make it new.**

Are you flirting?

—**Not very well, if you must ask.**

:) I am yawning like crazy. I better get to sleep.

— **Bonne nuit!**

You too.

She scrolled through the few texts they'd shared before turning off the light. Nothing profound, yet the loneliness of Chartres faded. The photo April had sent of the Eiffel Tower sign came to mind. A kiss on the cheek would be appropriate. As she faded into sleep, she dreamed of more.

How was a guy supposed to flirt by text? He had rarely texted Justine unless a meeting or fitting had run long. André needed to figure out flirt texting if the long-distance relationship was going to have a chance. The time change was just enough to make communication difficult, especially with Gina working for a company with a no-cell-phone policy—a policy he should implement in the fashion-design studio.

He set his phone on the worktable and studied the gown on the dress form. The dress was to the point he wanted to do a fitting, but that wasn't possible. He went in search of Grand-mère and Marie.

The two sat in front of the television again, critiquing the clothing on an American reality show and eating macarons.

"I wonder if you two can take a break to look at a real dress."

"Are you going to model it?" Marie laughed.

André rolled his eyes and helped them up from their seats. Grand-mère leaned on his arm as he escorted them to the workroom.

"Très belle!" Marie clapped her hands.

Grand-mère walked around the dress, studying it from every angle. "May I see my sketch?"

André handed her the book.

"How much of the silk do you have left?" She sat at the table.

"Not quite two meters."

Grand-mère's pencil flew over the page. "Do you have enough to create this?"

André measured the silk, then cut a piece of plain muslin to the same dimensions as the silk and wrapped the cloth over the skirt of the dress, careful not to damage the silk or lace. "I have enough." André set the cloth on the table and picked up a remnant of the lace he'd used on the bodice. "What if the roses and vines were appliqued here?"

"They would need beading."

"Swarovski crystal or onyx?"

Grand-mère ran her finger along the outline of the rose. "Crystal. Also around these three roses in the bodice." She pointed to the gown on the form.

André glanced at the clock. He wasn't nearly as proficient at handwork as he should be. If only he had access to the seamstresses at work.

Marie cleared her throat. "My fingers are not as nimble as they were years ago, but I can still hold a needle." Some of her work graced Grand-mère's own dresses. Even half her best would outshine his work any day.

André kissed her on both cheeks. "You must have been reading my mind."

Grand-mère harrumphed. "It wasn't hard to do. All the color drained from your face. Cut out the applique section for the skirt first. Marie, my black Swarovski crystal beads are in the third drawer down of my bead cabinet. There should be enough. If we take any from the studio, Arabelle will wonder, and I don't want her snooping."

"I have over a hundred in my collection in my office. Arabelle won't know they are gone. I can bring them tomorrow." André laid out the lace on some waxed parchment to use as a temporary stabilizer.

Marie left, presumably in search of the beads. Grand-mère flipped through the pages of her book. "Merci, André, for bringing an old woman's doodles to life. It has been so long since anything of mine has been taken from paper to fabric."

"I just hope I do your creation justice."

Grand-mère kissed André on each cheek. "You will, mon trésor."

She shuffled out of the room. He should not have stayed away for so long.

Gina hurried along the damp streets. On the map, the Eiffel Tower looked closer to Musée d'Orsay than it was. If she hadn't looked so long at the van Gogh paintings, she would not have had to hurry through Cézanne and Degas. Either way, she was going to be twenty minutes late for her ticket time. She wound through the entrance line at the tower, glad to have a prepaid ticket and time. She exchanged her reservation for a ticket, all the while searching for André. They'd only made plans for if he were late. Ticket in hand, she waited in another line for a security check before waiting in yet another line for the elevator to take her to the second level. Still no sign of André.

Standing in line for the elevator for the second level.

No reply.

Gina entered the elevator with a couple dozen tourists from at least six different countries. Tourists crowded the lower floor of the second level. People all wanting to say they ate at the Eiffel Tower formed a line outside the restaurant. Gina read the various placards and history before walking around the crowded balcony. The lower floor of the second level was less crowded. But still no André.

Below, the Seine flowed serenely, reflecting the blue of the sky back to Gina. Raindrops glistened on every surface, making the entire city sparkle. A family, perhaps from Denmark, gathered around one of the binocular viewers, the youngest son pointing in awe. Gina passed them to find her own spot by the railing. Tourists bumped past her, raising their cameras and phones. Never had she seen so many selfie sticks, but then, she didn't usually frequent the tourist areas of New York unless she had a visiting cousin or college friend. Behind her, a tourist rudely extended one of the sticks over her left shoulder so close the pole brushed her hair, but instead of a phone, the stick held a single red rose. Gina whirled and tripped—into André's arms. He caught her without letting go of the stick.

Gina turned and reached for the flower. "That is the best use of one of those I've seen all day."

André turned to a group of Asian tourists and handed one of the men the selfie stick. "Merci."

Holding the rose close, Gina smiled while the tourists clicked photos of them. André took her hand and led her away from the group. "Can you do a few stairs? We can walk down to the first level. It is less crowded."

André needed a new definition for "a few." Gina raised her brows when they reached the first landing. "Do you always underestimate?"

"If I'd said 341, would you have come?"

"You gave me a rose on the Eiffel Tower using a selfie stick. I'd follow you twice that far." Gina followed him down a few more steps. No one else followed them, preferring the elevators.

André stopped halfway down and turned around. They stood eye to eye. The green of his eyes reflected more blue as he reached up and traced a finger down the side of her face. "This is the most private spot in this very public place. Stair number 511. Kiss me?" He stood only a breath away, not moving any closer.

No one had ever asked to kiss her before. Until that moment, she'd never understood the tenderness behind such a request. If one of her friends told her their boyfriend asked for a kiss, she would have laughed. Instead, Gina raised her hand to André's face, leaned in, and brushed a kiss across his lips. The steps started to vibrate as a herd of teenagers raced down the stairs above them.

André turned and descended the steps again. Gina followed. The stairs were wide enough, but she didn't want to be passed by the rowdy group, fearing she might fall over the railing. She and André reached the first level a few steps before the thundering herd came down behind them. As the group took off in one direction, André led her in another. Only a couple people stood on this balcony. Gina noted that they now stood in one of the pink kissing-spot circles.

André bent to whisper in her ear. "I liked our spot better."

"How did you know that was step 511/12?"

"I don't. I just know the one at the top of the second level is labeled 669. We could go back and count them."

"No, thank you. I declare you are right." There was no one between them and the next corner.

"Waltz?"

Before Gina could answer, André spun her into his arms and started whirling her along the balcony in a one-two-three rhythm. Gina laughed as they twirled. Sky, city, and iron flashed in her peripheral vision as she focused on André's smile and eyes. Next to the south leg of the tower, they stopped, and he dipped her á la Fred Astaire. As he pulled her out of the dip, their lips met. More than a mere brush, this kiss connected two souls just as with hundreds, maybe thousands, of others on the same tower for more than a century.

Gina held on to André for balance for a second when the kiss ended. She smiled up at him, took his hand, and they explored the rest of the level. They found another of the pink circles. André kissed her on each cheek while standing in it. Gina was glad it wasn't a lover's kiss, not where everyone else was standing to record their moment with a selfie stick.

"Have dinner with me?"

"As long as it isn't up there." Gina pointed in the general direction of the restaurant on the second level.

"Definitely not. But someday we will go up to the top level."

Someday. Future plans. Gina smiled. "Elevator both ways. In fact, we better take it, or I might not be able to walk tomorrow."

"Planning on walking a lot tomorrow?"

"Of course. Isn't that the only way to see Paris?"

"I wish I could see the city with you. But there are details for Monday's party that have fallen to me. However, Sunday I am all yours if you wish."

"I wish that very much."

They shared another kiss in a sheltered corner before finding the elevator. Gina adjusted her bag as they followed the crowd in. When April asked, Gina would tell her she'd stood in the circle and received a traditional cheek kiss from the most handsome Frenchman in Paris.

By noon on Saturday, André wished for a fairy godmother to finish the dress, though Marie's beading and sewing had saved him hours of frustration. The underskirt proved to be the biggest chore. Neither Grand-mère nor he had enough of the lightweight material in black. Taking a few meters from the roll in the work-room at Galli-Batiste didn't go as planned when he interrupted a meeting of Arabelle and some other designers.

"André, I didn't think I invited you." His cousin folded her arms and glared.

"Neither did I." Distrust filled the room like cigar smoke. André greeted each of the five designers by name. None of them divulged what had brought them out before noon on a Saturday to huddle around a worktable, and André didn't ask.

Arabelle kept her arms crossed. "Did you need something?"

"Elinore needs a few yards of material."

A collective gasp rose from the table. "She still sews?" asked Pierre, a forty-something designer who had been with them for over twenty years and had his name on his own sub-collection.

"Non, but she still designs. I assume her creativity is the secret to her longevity." André hoped the vague answer would be enough.

"Don't let us stop you, then," spat Arabelle. "And don't forget to enter what you take in the computer as personal use. Accounting gets upset when goods go missing."

André nodded. Four years ago, he'd implemented the current policy to curb a rash of disappearing materials. The finest of the fabrics were stored in a room accessed only by ID badges. With some of the fabrics costing upward of one hundred euros a meter, they'd saved thousands of euros a year in missing supplies.

Five meters of the lining was more than enough for two dresses. André took that much anyway, assuming Arabelle would check the logs. He added two meters of tulle and some inexpensive notions just to make her wonder. He considered taking two meters of a hideous tangerine satin that had been collecting dust since 1998. However, he didn't want rumors circulating. He slowly gathered his things, but the designers only gossiped about other design houses' summer collections. André left the building wondering if any of them would clue him in later. He'd let his father know next time he saw him.

The meeting didn't surprise Grand-mère. "She is moving so quickly. I hoped my threat of keeping things quiet until I made the announcement would keep Arabelle in check through the weekend."

"But you have no proof she told them anything."

"But I will. Kindness makes for loyal employees. There are some who think I am not an old relic and come for macarons and tea more often than you think. The tulle is an excellent idea. I should have realized the gown needed some." Grand-mère left him alone to work.

His phone pinged. Gina.

— How is your day?

Busier than I planned. Trying to finish up things I thought would take less time to do. André stood back and admired the dress. A few of the seams in the bodice remained basted. He could finish those tomorrow after Gina tried it on.

—Most work tasks taking longer than I want them to.

And your day?

— I met Nick and Zoe for lunch. We took two hours. I could get used to the biggest-meal-of-the-day-for-lunch thing.

I missed it in the US.

— We are going shopping now.

Getting anything fun?

— I need some shoes for Monday. I am borrowing Zoe's black dress, but her feet are smaller than mine. Mostly just window shopping. I wish we would have been able to get a fourth ticket tonight.

Enjoy your dinner cruise! André's disappointment at not getting a ticket was tempered by the fact that the only appealing part of being on the cruise was Gina. A decade ago, he'd entertained far too many visitors by taking them on cruises. By the tenth one, he'd vowed never again. A vow he would have broken for Gina.

Pierre visited Grand-mère late in the afternoon. André shut the door to the workroom as the conversation carried on. Arabelle's plans must be desperate to have the senior designer showing up within just hours of the meeting. Hopefully, they could wait until another day to deal with whatever was going on.

André put away the broom as the clock struck midnight. He considered sleeping in one of the spare rooms, but the need to change clothing in the morning before picking up Gina for their Sunday outing and lunch with Grand-mère won out.

18

Gina adjusted the scarf again, then ran into the bathroom. Ever since her first date to a movie when she was a sophomore in high school, her nerves would send her running to the bathroom a half dozen times on false alarms. Half a lifetime later, the psychosomatic symptom still haunted her. Gina checked the peephole when a light knock sounded on her door. It wasn't a maid this time. The false alarm twenty minutes ago had had her smearing lipstick across her face.

She opened the door. André handed her a single pink rose. Gina smelled it.

"How do you do that?" He leaned against the doorframe.

"What?"

André brushed her cheek with his thumb. "Blush the same color as the rose?" He kissed her on both cheeks before brushing a kiss across her lips. "I missed you yesterday."

Gina felt her cheeks heat more. No way they were the same color as the rose. "I missed you too. Did you get everything done?"

André nodded. "Shall we go? I wanted to take you to one of my favorite parks before we go to Grand-mère's."

"Did I tie this correctly?" Gina touched the scarf.

"There isn't one correct way, and I like the style on you." His smile tempted her to go in for another kiss. However, she had set some strict rules about kissing a man in her hotel room, and they'd come as close as she dared to the safety lines she made for relationships already.

André drove towards his grand-mère's in yet another vehicle, a black sedan this time. He alternated holding her hand and using two hands to drive. They parked in the garage below the apartment and left through the side door.

"The park is close enough to walk. In case you haven't noticed, parking in Paris is harder to find than in New York."

Gina took his hand and interlaced their fingers. "I assume that accounts for French cars being half the size of American. You can fit twice as many in a parking lot." A week ago, she would have cared more about the history of the park Central Park was modeled after. Today she only cared about the man next to her. André told stories of coming to the park with his grand-père and of his first kite and boat ride. At the docks he rented a boat, and they rowed out to the island.

"When I was about six, I thought it would be grand to stay on the island all night. I sneaked out and came down here only to discover the proprietor locked up the boats at night. Never had a child known such devastation. Grand-père found me curled up near the boathouse. The next weekend, he took me out in the country on my first camping trip."

"Dad would take us to a cabin on a little lake in Vermont each summer. We still try to get together for family reunions in the area. Now that there are spouses and grandchildren, we need more space."

They returned to the dock. Gina checked her clothing to make sure she hadn't soiled anything and replaced the scarf she'd stored inside the clean zipper quart bag she kept in her purse for such circumstances. "Does it look all right?"

André untied the ends and pulled Gina closer. "Hmm ..." He adjusted the scarf a couple times. "I think I like this knot best." He tugged on the ends, bringing their faces together. The kiss ended before any of the people around them took notice. "Very useful, n'est ce pas?"

"Too bad you don't have on a tie. I could reciprocate." Gina patted his chest.

Her statement was met with a laugh. "I'll remember that during my next boring meeting when I am contemplating my tie."

Back at Elinore's, they were met by delicious smells the moment Marie opened the door.

"Five minutes until lunch. Elinore is in the parlor."

Elinore clapped her hands when she saw them. "I am so pleased you chose one of my favorites."

They exchanged greetings the French way. Gina found she liked it almost as well as a hug.

The four-course meal lasted over an hour and a half as they conversed over half a dozen topics, from the scheduled train strikes to which of the two closest bakeries made the better croissants. Elinore had a surprising knowledge of American reality television. At the end of the meal, Marie cleared the cheese-and-fruit plates.

"Now for the best part. André, the sketchbook, please." Elinore flipped through the pages of the small black leather book he handed her. "Last Sunday when you were here, I sketched a little thing. I named the gown "The Century Dress." Although I assume it is probably the last gown I'll design, labeling the sketch as such will only stifle my creativity." Elinore set the book down in front of Gina.

"Oh. That is exquisite." The curly mane of hair on the faceless model looked a bit like what greeted her in the mirror each morning.

"I asked André to construct it for me. I think he did a fair job considering he hasn't sewn these last five years. I long to see someone model it. Would you try the dress on?"

"I am hardly a model's height or size."

"Most women aren't, *chérie*. Come see." Elinore stood and entered a back hallway André hadn't shown her on the tour. "This is my personal workroom. Granted, I haven't sewn anything since 2005, but I have had others make clothing for me here."

A huge table filled one side of the room. Drawers and cupboards lined the walls. At one end, two sewing machines and a serger sat. In the far corner stood a screen. There was no dress.

Elinore sat in a chair and nodded to André, who moved the folding screen back to reveal a deep-blue dress with black lace—the sketch in 3-D. Gina sucked in a breath.

"Look closer. It won't bite."

Gina circled the dress. On a low table sat a clutch purse made of the same fabric and two black shoes covered in the same beads scattered across the gown. She turned to André. "You sewed this?"

"Fashion is in my DNA. Grand-mère had me sewing for spending money when I was a teen."

"This is what you were doing yesterday?"

"Guilty. Try it on."

"How could this dress fit me?"

"On Tuesday the dress I had you fit for the tour—it was the base for this dress. I also took your measurements from the computer file."

"Oh!"

He knew her waist size in centimeter, as well as her—

"The silk is some I found on one of my buying trips. The lace came from Grand-mère's collection." He gestured to some of the closed cabinets. "She designed the gown for you."

"But I can't—"

"Just try it on. Marie will help you."

"But—"

André and Elinore left the room, ignoring her protests.

Marie had a black slip over one arm. "Go behind the screen

and put this on. Then I will help you with the dress. Some of the seams are, how do you say it …busted?"

"You mean basted?"

"Yes, basted. Tonight, André will fix, and tomorrow you can put this on yourself."

Gina held her arms up as Marie slipped the dress over her head, zipped up the side zipper, and straightened the skirt. The room had no mirror. Gina wanted to know if the dress looked as divine as it felt.

Marie held up the shoes. Gina balanced on one foot at a time to put them on. They too fit perfectly.

"Come."

Gina followed her out of the room, searching for a mirror.

It was a tie. Grand-mère's expression of joy versus Gina in the dress.

"*Magnifique!* Oh, André!" Grand-mère kissed him on the cheek, then turned and kissed Gina on both. "Merci. To see my creation on a real woman—you do not know what this means to me. You must wear the dress tomorrow night as your birthday gift to me."

Gina opened her mouth, thinking she might protest, when André held out his hand. "Come look in the mirror."

Gina won. Her expression of pure wonder plus the gown earned her at least two extra points.

"How is it this dress can make me feel taller and thinner than I was only ten minutes ago?"

"Grand-mère says a woman's clothes should always make her feel that way. There are a couple seams I want to adjust."

"This dress is too much. I can't …"

André set his hands on her shoulders. "Every woman deserves a Cinderella moment or two in her life, and Grand-mère wants to play the role of the fairy godmother. Let her do this."

Gina held his gaze for a few moments. "If she is the fairy god-mother, what does that make you? My Prince Charming or one of the worker mice?"

"Perhaps a little of both. Cinderella didn't kiss the mice." André leaned into brush his lips against hers.

Grand-mère cleared her throat, and André stepped back. "You need a final touch." Grand-mère held out a velvet box. "I would like to loan you these."

Gina gasped at the sight of the diamond earrings and necklace. "Too much. Way too much." She stepped back.

"These are only a loan. I will have my bodyguard bring them so you need not worry about keeping them at your hotel."

Gina nodded. "That makes me feel better."

"Try them on."

André took the necklace and fastened it behind her neck. There was a kissable spot right above the clasp, but it would have to wait until Grand-mère wasn't watching. Gina took out her silver hoops and replaced them with the diamonds. "I feel like a princess."

"And you look like one."

"Do an old woman a favor. Use this room for what it was meant. Dance for me?"

André whispered to Gina. "How is your waltz?"

"Fair."

"Find some music on your phone. I'll move a couple of the tables."

"No need for a phone. I have the music right here." Grand-mère held up a remote and clicked it. The first notes of a big-band-era song filled the air. André spun Gina into position and waltzed her around the room. This was how the prince fell in love, gazing into the eyes of his princess. After the third song, André bowed to his grand-mère, and Gina curtsied. "If you will excuse us, I need to adjust a couple seams."

André didn't let go of Gina's hand. Hidden speakers delivered the music to the workroom, where André pulled Gina into his arms and spun her one time before claiming the kiss he wanted to for the past half hour. Gina's hand covered his heart and remained linked with his own. The music stopped, and they pulled apart. Gina ducked her head. André lifted her chin with one finger. "Why are you blushing?"

"I was just thinking about Cinderella." She stepped back. "Which seams did you want to fix?"

André took out a small pedestal and helped Gina up. The hem dipped in a spot it shouldn't, and a seam near the waist needed a half centimeter taken out of it. "Finished. Can you get out of the dress on your own, or do you need Marie's assistance?"

"If you will take Elinore's jewelry and help with the zipper, I think I can manage."

André left the room with the diamond necklace and earrings. Perhaps one day they would be hers.

It was pointless to try to sightsee on Monday morning. Gina gave up after an hour and texted Zoe.

Can I get ready at your place?

—Sure. I was wondering when you were going to come get my dress.

Sorry, I forgot to tell you—Elinore designed me one. She had lost several rounds of Scrabble played in both French and English with Elinore and Marie while André adjusted the dress. After the third time he made her try the dress on, she teased him that he just liked to kiss her when she wore it. He'd proven otherwise on their circuitous route back to her hotel. They took selfies on the Pont des Arts bridge, where lovers used to leave padlocks until the city removed them a few years ago. Now they left them on other bridges across the Seine.

—What!?!?!? I'll be at the apartment at noon. Be there and be prepared to spill.

I'll be there.

Gina texted André next.

Please pick me up at Nick and Zoe's instead of the hotel.

— You told her?

Just about the dress.

—Can you be ready a half hour earlier? Grand-mère asked if you could finish at her place, then have her chauffeur take the four of us and my dad over at the same time.

I am meeting your father?

— Yes.

I guess I would have at the party, too. I'll be ready.

— I can't wait, ma chérie.

Moi aussi.

Last night André had started using more French in their conversations, pointing out that if their relationship were to grow, she'd need to dust off her college French and learn to speak like a local. His point was valid. While she could continue her artwork in Paris, every artist's dream, he could not always work in the States as eventually he would take over his father's role. André hedged on that point but admitted it had been discussed since he was a toddler.

Gina's phone beeped. Zoe.

—Hey, we are driving back to apartment now. Do you need us to pick you up? A dress and makeup, etc., would be a pain to walk the two blocks with.

Just arriving at hotel now. Thanks. I didn't want to call a cab. I understand they are hard to get because of regulations.

— Be there in ten.

Gina only waited a moment in the lobby before the chauffeured car pulled up. Considering she had her backpack, small travel bag, and the garment bag André gave her with the dress in it, Gina was more than happy to have help from the driver.

Zoe bounced in the seat next to Nick.

Not wanting to talk in front of the driver or Nick, Gina started the conversation in hopes of keeping Zoe talking. "So, what is your favorite thing you've seen so far?"

"Gargoyles. Now spill."

Gina shook her head. "Nick, what about you?"

"My favorite thing has been watching Zoe try to pretend she isn't a tourist while awed by everything she sees."

Zoe elbowed Nick and rolled her eyes. The short drive ended, and the driver held the door for them as they exited the car.

Nick took Gina's backpack and bag up to the apartment. "I am as curious as Zoe. How on earth did you get Elinore to design you a dress? My mother will be so curious. Her wedding dress was an Elinore custom design, as was her 'going-away' dress."

Zoe led Gina to a spare bedroom with adjoining bath. "I didn't know that."

"It never came up." Nick set the bags on a chair.

"It should have. I mean, I borrowed her veil."

Nick shrugged. "I guess I assumed she told you. Most grooms don't discuss their bride's wedding dress—the whole bad-luck thing and all."

"That is if you see her in the dress that day. Anyway, it is Gina's gown we are discussing."

Gina told an abbreviated version of the story, excluding the dancing and kissing, while she laid out the dress and shoes.

Zoe sat on the end of the bed. "So, just how serious are things with André?"

Nick interrupted. "I'm going to leave for the rest of the girl talk. I have some things I can take care of business-wise. Not that my opinion matters, but I did find André to be an honest man to work with when I was working on his real-estate issues in Manhattan. Not everyone I meet in his position has integrity." Nick left them alone.

Zoe raised a brow. "So?"

"We are talking about how a long-distance relationship might work. It does help that he just closed on an apartment in the Plaza a couple floors below yours. And he claims to have a gazillion frequent-flyer miles, so I don't feel guilty about flying over here."

"For what it is worth, you look happy. I don't think I have ever seen you so relaxed. I didn't realize the tightness around your eyes was there. Now, how can I help?"

"How are you at updos?"

"I didn't get to be runner-up at the county fair without learning a few tricks. How long is your hair?"

Gina stretched a curl near her shoulder out, the lock reaching halfway down her front."

Zoe clapped. "Do you have a robe? If not, there is one in the bathroom. Go shower, and we'll let the fun begin."

How many fairy godmothers does a woman need?

Gina wasn't going to turn down any of them.

André chose a classic tuxedo cut rather than one of the newer looks from the Galli-Batiste line. There would be enough attention coming his way once Grand-mère made her announcement. She'd limited the press presence to the executive editor of *Le Monde* newspaper, a correspondent for the BBC, and one photographer in her employ who would disseminate the official photos, but this wouldn't bar cell phones. Critics would comment regardless of what he wore, but there would be little to comment on about his classic look. He checked his cuff links again. The pair had once belonged to Grand-père. Wearing them tonight seemed fitting.

The driver picked him up promptly. His father was already in the car.

"Elinore tells me she has another surprise for tonight. She wants me to see it before the celebration. She was rather vague, even for her. Any idea what she is up to?"

"Grand-mère designed a dress for a friend of mine who has become somewhat more this week. It has been a few years since she designed a custom dress from the pages of her sketchbook, and I think she is more excited than the woman wearing it." The car stopped in front of Nick's apartment. "Her name is Gina Swann, and she's from New York."

André exited the car before his father could respond.

Nick answered the door. "She'll be out in a moment. My mother would be green with envy. I don't know if Gina understands the significance."

"She does. The shock took a couple hours to wear off."

Zoe entered the living area, phone in hand. "May I get a photo of the two of you? Don't worry—just for Gina, not social media."

"Oui."

Gina came into the room, her hair up. The simple change added a layer of elegance. André couldn't help but bow. "Mademoiselle, your carriage awaits."

Gina took the phone from Zoe. "Thanks for putting my things back in my room."

Zoe hugged her friend and whispered something André couldn't hear. "Have a good evening."

André assisted Gina into the vehicle. "Père, this is Gina Swann. We met in New York." Explaining that the relationship only spanned the time Gina had toured Paris would not start the evening off well.

His father nodded. "Mathieu Batiste. Delighted to meet the woman who has my son designing again."

Gina blushed. "Nice to meet you."

The driver navigated the roads while André pointed out some of his favorite spots. "I forgot how enjoyable using a driver can be." He squeezed Gina's hand. If Justine had used a driver, perhaps she might still be alive. But then he would have never met the woman beside him. Compatible and even companionable described what their relationship had been, but there was a certain *je ne sais quoi* that was always missing. They both felt it, yet neither one discussed the lack of love in their marriage merger. One of the few topics he hadn't discussed with Gina was the night his uncle had crashed Justine's car, killing them both. Neither should have been driving. And they shouldn't have been together. Rumors of affairs on both their parts had circulated for months, or, on his uncle's part, years. Three wives had testified to his lack of fidelity. André never believed Justine could choose a man twice her age. Tonight wasn't the night. A video chat would be easier and detached. Perhaps he could tell the story without blaming himself. If he'd stayed at the party or hired a driver...

"Are you worried about something?" Gina interrupted his thoughts.

"No, just remembering something I'd rather not."

"Oh." She furrowed her brows.

"It is a conversation for another night." He hoped his smile was convincing.

Grand-mère stood in her parlor. Her dress took years off her age.

Gina greeted Grand-mère with a kiss to each cheek.

Grand-mère patted the spot next to her on the sofa. "I need to prepare you a little for tonight. Someone had the horrid idea of doing a retrospective fashion show to start off the evening. I would like you to go last."

The color drained from Gina's face, but she made no protest.

"Don't worry. André will escort you as long as you can walk a straight line. Holding on to his arm, you'll do just fine. I only learned of the show this afternoon or I would have warned you sooner. There will be mingling, etc. Most of the guests will leave, and we will have dinner. At dinner I will announce André as the new president of Galli-Batiste International."

Gina looked to André. He nodded.

"Good. He didn't tell you. I nearly said something yesterday, but I am afraid I needed to keep the information secret, as I forbade the board from discussing it. Now, for your jewels." Grand-mère turned to the burly security guard in the corner of the room and nodded him forward. "This is Jean-Paul. He has been with me for at least thirty years."

Jean-Paul presented a velvet box.

"When you are ready to leave for the evening, find Jean-Paul and return your jewels." Grand-mère didn't mention the team would know where Gina and the necklace were at all times. Gina would faint if she knew the value of the heirloom.

Gina held the necklace out to André. He fastened the clasp, an easier task with her hair in the updo.

Grand-mère adjusted the scarf on her coral gown as she stood.

"Did you design this one, too?" André kissed his Grand-mère, something he'd neglected to do earlier.

"Non, I held a little competition among the designers six months ago. As I recall, you didn't submit one. Pierre submitted this one. I did not want the pressure of wearing my own gown and having the other designers gossip that I didn't dress my age or something equally ridiculous. Mathieu Batiste, your arm, please. Your son's is occupied."

André showed Gina how to lay her arm on top of his in the regency style they would use at the end of the fashion show. "This way they can see the entire dress."

"I nearly died when she told me," she whispered, leaning in toward him. "I am so glad you will be at my side. Did you know?"

"This is the first I heard of the retrospective as well. I don't think Grand-mère is pleased." André helped her into the car. He and his father sat in the rear-facing seats.

Photographers lined the entrance to the Musée de Rodin.

André leaned forward and took Gina's hand. "Ready?"

His heart somersaulted at the brave smile she gave him. Gina's willingness to put other's pleasure before her own brought him new joy.

20

The photographers had been absent in the daydreams Gina had concocted of the party. Ahead of them, Elinore nodded and waved to the well-wishers. Gina concentrated on smiling, breathing, and not falling off her shoes. André tucked her a bit closer into his side. "Ma chérie, merci for this."

The emotion rolling off him was potent enough to have her kissing him, even if there were hundreds of people watching and photographing. *Qui est-elle?* came from the paparazzi shouting to know Gina's identity.

"Ma chérie." André waved with his free hand, then propelled them to the entrance, where they posed before going in.

"Why did you say that?"

"Because it's true, and I wasn't about to feed you completely to the wolves."

Gina blinked. *Love* wasn't a word bantered about easily in American culture. Did the use of it signify the same in his?

André mingled and introduced her to people with names she had seen in the stores lining Fifth Avenue. Most of them studied her dress. When they had a second between greetings, André whispered, "They are all trying to figure out who designed your dress. But they won't ask. Not here."

"I thought they were trying to decide who the woman too short to be a model on your arm was."

"I think you are the perfect height. Shall I find us a private corner and prove it?" He raised his brows.

Heat flooded her face. "Perhaps later."

"There are a couple of sculptures we could imitate."

"Like that one." Gina nodded to *The Thinker*.

"Not exactly what I have in mind."

A delicious shiver traveled up her spine.

"André!" A woman grasped him by the shoulders and pressed herself against him as she greeted him with a not-so-traditional kiss on each cheek.

"Celine, it's nice to see you." André extricated himself from the woman's hold. "May I introduce my girlfriend, Gina."

The tall blonde spoke with a heavy accent. "André, a girlfriend? Do you think you can replace my sister?"

"It's been more than three years. I think it is time we all move on." Meaning that spoke of a long history and a warning infused his voice.

"You need to be in the tent at the far end of the garden in ten minutes. We want to get the show over before those clouds ruin the day. At least you don't need your hair done."

"Celine, we will be there."

The woman sashayed off.

"Sorry about that. She has spent the last five years trying to prove I married the wrong woman. All she did was keep me away from women altogether."

Was Justine like that? Gina didn't voice her question.

"I'll save the story for one of our long-distance phone calls. I don't want to ruin our evening with the tale of Celine chasing me."

Gina smiled to cover her questions. At least he was willing to discuss his dead wife. They wandered in the direction of the tent, where André's cousin stood at the door. "About time. We are almost ready to begin." She turned to Gina. "Head down the marked path past the back of the building, and pause and turn at each corner and in front of where the VIPs are sitting." Arabelle didn't look at Gina as she spoke, but at least she spoke in English. "Celine will give you your cue. André, you can go sit with Elinore."

"Grand-mère was very specific. She wanted me to escort Miss Swann."

Arabelle rolled her eyes. "Probably just as well. I doubt Gina has ever seen a fashion show, let alone modeled before." Arabelle walked off to the far corner of the tent before Gina could correct her assumptions.

"Remind me to tell her I have been designing programs for years for the New York fashion week and have attended several shows …Sorry, that was catty."

André laughed. "I'm surprised she didn't say something worse."

"Should we watch the walkway for trip wires?"

"And land mines."

The models left the tent, one for every year of Elinore's career. Each model held a sign with the year. Other than the unfortunate jumpsuit from 1972, Gina found each outfit as elegant as the rest.

Beside her, André growled. "Grand-mère hated that one and several of the others." It is as if Celine went out of her way to show the designs Grand-mère detested most. If she wants to keep her position, she is not doing a good job of showing it. She could leave with Arabelle.

"Only one looked out of place to me."

"1972. Ready?" André laid her arm on top of his as they practiced. They left exactly fifteen steps behind 2012—the last year Elinore designed a manufactured collection.

"Breathe and look forward." His lips didn't move. Gina would ask about his ventriloquist skills later.

At the first corner, André turned her as he had in their waltz yesterday. The second turn was the same. In front of the pavilion where Elinore sat, they stopped and faced the crowd.

An unseen announcer spoke in French. "Mesdames et Messieurs, Elinore Galli's latest creation—the Century Dress, designed exclusively for Miss Gina Swann of New York." André led her in a slow circle to a standing ovation.

Elinore joined them, lacing her arm through André's free one. "*Merci, mes amis.* Thank you all for attending my celebration. It looks like the rain will descend upon us at any moment. Let us go inside and enjoy the sculptures, which are decidedly older than me." The crowd clapped again.

"André, take us inside."

The first drop of rain hit Gina only feet from the door. "That was perfect timing."

"Perfect timing would have been if they'd never had the charade of a fashion show in the first place. Arabelle was in rare form tonight." Elinore frowned.

"If you'll excuse me, I need to go powder my nose." Gina smiled.

André smiled at her old-fashioned term and nodded at the hallway to the right.

In the tiny stall, Gina gathered the skirt of the gown in the under slip, glad for doors reaching to the floor. A couple of women came in speaking rapidly in French. Gina did her best to translate.

"I thought the old bat …take the bait and make the announcement while …seated."

"Choosing some of the ugliest dresses from her collections … not endear you to her. Isn't she still on the board?"

"…few more hours, …I have André to deal with."

"Have you decided …?"

"Most of the designers …with me in the fall …almost impossible for him …a collection for next February …talk will resurface … him …responsible for the death …sister and my stepfather." The speakers must be Celine and Arabelle.

"He …murdered them," hissed one of the women. "…American gold …on his arm?"

"How could I miss it, and the gown.... Elinore ...drop dead ... she still has talent."

"...a plan for tonight ..."

The women left.

Gina processed the parts of the conversation she understood. André had killed his wife? Party or not, she needed to find him. Now.

André continued to escort Grand-mère until Père found them.

"There isn't a designer in Paris who isn't drooling over Gina's gown. Two designers asked me where the silk came from. I'm glad I could honestly plead ignorance." Mathieu Batiste chuckled.

André left them in search of Gina.

Well-wishers stopped his progress every few feet. He rounded a corner into Celine's arms.

She didn't move back. "Darling, there you are. Where did your little Ginny go?"

"*Gina* will be back soon." André stepped away.

"You can't be serious about her. An American. What would my sister say?" Celine advanced.

"Celine, your sister never loved me. Stop this right now." He turned to go, but she moved into his path.

"So you admit you drove her to it? You are the reason she is dead?"

This conversation was not happening in the middle of the gallery. André stepped into a vacant corridor. "Justine made her own choices. I asked her to come home with me, and she refused. We have been through this before. All the answers died with her and my uncle. Now, if you will excuse me—"

Celine lunged forward, grabbing him around the neck, and dove in for an intimate kiss.

André put his hands on her waist and pushed her back.

Celine gave a satisfied smile and walked off. André turned to see Gina on the stairway landing below them, hand over her mouth. She gathered her skirt and ran down the stairs.

"Gina!"

She disappeared. André made it two steps before one of their top competitors stopped him. By the time he found his way down the stairs, he couldn't find her.

21

A security guard stood near the main doorway.
"*Ou est Jean-Paul?*"

The man pointed to the exterior of the building where a car was leaving with some guests.

Gina burst through the door, removing the earrings. "I must go." She handed him the jewels and tried to work the clasp on the necklace. She needed to leave before André could find her. A man who would kill his wife and then lock lips with her sister when he was dating someone else! The necklace came loose, and she thrust it into Jean-Paul's hand. "Taxi?"

"Take that car." He pointed to the next black sedan in line.

Gina hopped in the car before the driver could help her. "*Alez vite*! Hurry!" She told the driver the name and street of her hotel.

As they drove, she checked her app to find the next flight to New York. The last flight of the day left at 18:30. It was after 6:00 p.m. The flight would be boarding now. Her phone pinged.

—**Where are you? Let me explain. I didn't kiss her.**

Tears pooled in her eyes. How many of her old boyfriends had tried to explain themselves after being caught doing what they shouldn't? She turned her attention back to the app. There was a flight at seven in the morning. The driver stopped at the hotel.

Gina paid his fee on her credit card and hopped out. Zoe stood by the elevator with Gina's bags.

"Gina, what's wrong? You're back early."

Gina pushed the already lit elevator button, willing the two-person elevator down from the third floor. A man and his wife exited.

"Why, aren't you lovely, dear." The wife spoke with a British accent.

Gina gave her a tight smile and got into the elevator with Zoe. "I am taking the first flight I can get on back to New York. I am glad you are here. You can return the dress to André."

"What? Why?"

The tears she had held back streamed down her face. "Because I thought I could have my Cinderella moment."

"If you just ran away from André, then I'd say you did."

Zoe's humor was not appreciated. Gina unlocked the door. "Can you help me get this off?"

Her phone pinged.

"I bet it is André. You should answer it."

"No! If I had $100 for every guy who has ever wanted to 'explain,' and another hundred every time I believed him, I could afford this dress. I'm thirty-three years old. I've spent half of my life dating. He was kissing her. I should have never—"

Zoe pulled the gown over Gina's head. "Maybe he has a logical explanation. Like in the movies where some girl corners the guy and kisses him just to make the other one jealous."

"That's in the movies. It doesn't happen in real life. And then he is responsible for his wife's death. I can't marry a guy who killed his wife."

"Whoa there, girl. Slow down. I thought a drunk-driving accident killed his wife."

Gina hiccupped and nodded as she pulled on her favorite jeans. "Was he driving?"

Gina mumbled a no as she pulled on a shirt.

"Then he didn't kill her. Perhaps you heard wrong."

"They were talking in French, but I heard *meurtre*, which means murder; *femme*, meaning wife; *oncle*; and *responsable*. I can understand French better than I can speak it. Not that it matters. I'm never coming back, not even to see the *Mona Lisa* without one of my headaches." Gina tossed her things in her suitcase, along with the few souvenirs she'd purchased. She put the dress in the bag and handed it to Zoe.

"Why are you packing now? There aren't any night flights to New York. I know. I checked when I booked ours."

The phone pinged again. Gina changed the mode to silent. "I need to trade my ticket in, and maybe they can find me something to Atlanta or anyplace. If I see him, I'll give in. I know I will, and the pain will only be worse next time. I was so stupid to let myself even dream we had something."

Zoe picked up Gina's shoes. "You are normally rational and well planned. Sit down and think this through."

"No. The longer I stay, the easier it is for him to find me. I need to go." Gina closed her disorganized suitcase and turned to her smaller bag, tossing in her makeup and toiletries.

Zoe sat on the suitcase. "Are you running from him or your feelings for him?"

Gina froze. "That isn't a fair question."

"Okay, next. There are no flights until morning. I doubt they'll let you hang out at the airport all night. Come to our place if you must check out of here, and I'll send you with a driver in the morning."

"He'll look there, and Nick won't lie. You know that. I'll go to the airport and ask about changing my ticket. If I can't fly out until morning, I'll get a hotel room out there."

"I still think you should talk to him."

"And I still can't. It is easier this way. He has a new position with Galli-Batiste . He won't be in New York very often. I won't have to see him again."

"So you are going to ghost him?"

"Zoe, please understand. This is the only way I can survive." Gina checked under the bed and in the bathroom. "Thank you for being a friend and for my ticket here. I wish I could stay, but I can't. I'll cry my way through Paris."

"At least let me send you with our driver to the airport. That way you won't end up lost on the train if you get a headache."

"You don't need to, but I've always hated taking my suitcase on the subway."

"Promise you'll at least text André so he knows you are safe?"

Gina didn't answer.

"Jean-Paul, have you seen Gina?" André found the guard seeing the last of the non-dinner guests out of the building.

"Monsieur Batiste, she left about a half hour ago. Don't worry. She gave me the earrings and necklace before she did."

The return of the jewels didn't concern him. "Merci."

Hoping to make his excuses and leave, André headed to the area where dinner would be served, texting Gina as he walked.

Jean-Paul said you left. Please let me know you are safe. I know what you thought you saw. Please give me a chance.

"There you are! Elinore is getting worried. She is making the announcement before the first course so she can kick the media out of the building." Père hurried his step, encouraging André to keep up. "Where is Gina?"

"She wasn't feeling well and left."

"I hope she didn't take the jewels. They are worth a small fortune."

"Jean-Paul said he had them."

All but a handful of guests sat at their assigned tables. He greeted Grand-mère with a kiss to each cheek and whispered in her ear. "Gina felt indisposed and left. Jean-Paul has your necklace."

"Tell me how she is doing as soon as you find out."

André took his seat next to Grand-mère. The seat that should be Gina's was filled by Arabelle. "I'm so sorry your little friend had to leave."

André nodded an acknowledgment, not wanting to start a conversation that would escalate into a fight.

Mathieu stood, microphone in hand. "It's my great honor to welcome you to a day few people ever celebrate. Elinore Galli's one-hundredth birthday, although she has reminded me a hundred times, she still has six days to go." The group laughed. "Before they serve our light meal, Elinore would like a few words."

"Fifty years ago, I never thought I would stand here talking to anyone, but then fifty years ago we landed on the moon, proving anything is possible. Tonight, I am retiring from the board of Galli-Batiste. I think as the oldest designer in the world, I've earned at least a few days of retirement." Chairs scraped on the floor as people stood and clapped. Grand-mère nodded and raised the microphone. "I'm not done yet." The clapping subsided. "There are a few last duties to perform. First, I would like to announce that Mathieu Batiste will retire at the end of the month, and effective May 1, his son, my grandson André, will become president of Galli-Batiste International." The room filled with applause again.

Grand-mère waited for silence. "I am glad to hear you approve of this as much as I do. Two more announcements, if you will bear with me. As you have seen tonight, I am not quite done designing. In the coming weeks, André will introduce a line based on designs I created over the past year. I should apologize for stealing his thunder, but one of the advantages of being a century old, I don't have to."

Laughter filled the room.

"And lastly, Arabelle Galli-Batiste has decided to leave and start her own fashion house."

Next to him, Arabelle spewed the water she was sipping.

"As many of you know, she is the stepdaughter of my son who

143

passed away three years ago. Arabelle, I wish you all the best in your new endeavor. Now for the part you are waiting for—the food." Grand-mère sat down with Mathieu's assistance.

Arabelle leaned across André and hissed at Elinore. "I never said I was leaving."

"Ah, but you did. I warned you—not one word about the change in president outside the boardroom. Saturday morning you informed several designers of the change. This evening you also discussed the takeover in the bathroom, along with scurrilous accusations against André. Since your meeting Saturday outlined plans for leaving Galli-Batiste and taking our designers with you, it seemed cleaner this way than just saying, as the Americans do, 'You're fired.'"

Arabelle pushed her chair back.

André stopped her with a hand on her leg. "If you leave now and cause a scene, you will do so in front of every top designer in the world. Look around the room. Is this what you really want to do?"

Arabelle scooted back into the table. "This isn't over."

Not by half. After being in the States for three years, gaining the other designers' loyalty will be difficult. Having them follow Arabelle would be a great way to clean house. André wondered who would stay.

Uniformed waiters served the soup, and quiet conversation filled the room.

André texted Gina again and again with no answer.

Grand-mère leaned near. "My source says Gina was in the ladies' room when Arabelle and Celine discussed ruining you by claiming you are responsible for your uncle's and Justine's deaths. How much French does Gina understand?"

So it wasn't just Celine's kiss that had sent Gina running. "Enough that she would pick up part of the conversation but not all of it."

"When are you going to go after her?"

"As soon as I can. I've been texting,"

"Face-to-face is always better, mon trésor."

"Then I will after tomorrow's press conferences. I don't think pounding on her hotel room door will work."

"Agreed, but don't wait too long."

By the time André got home, the bells on the church tower were sounding the first chimes of midnight. He called anyway and got voicemail. "Ma chérie, Grand-mère told me about what Arabelle and Celine said in the bathroom. I don't know how much you heard …Please let me explain face-to-face."

No answer came.

22

The 6:00 a.m. flight didn't leave Gina much time to sleep before returning to the airport. She never even changed clothes for the hour she slept in the hotel close to the airport. She debated calling André back but decided her flight left too early to hold the conversation he wanted, so she typed a text.

Returning to NYC this morning. Thank you for all the memories.

Her thumb hovered over the Send arrow. As they called her flight. She hit it and turned her phone off.

The only seats left on the morning flight were in coach. The business-class-ticket downgrade covered the cost of switching flights. Gina sat in the middle seat between a woman with pink-gray hair and a man with a comb-over and a stained suit coat. The woman's T-shirt proclaimed she was spending her grandchildren's inheritance seeing the world. The man studied every inch of Gina with dull, watery eyes. Gina plugged her earphones into the console in front of her, hoping to avoid conversation.

As the flight-safety video played, the man tapped her on the arm. Gina pulled out an earbud.

He handed her a business card. "Hi, I'm Stan the mattress man. How do you like to sleep?"

Gina put on her best French accent. "Je regret—"

"You don't fool me. I saw your passport when we boarded. Now, are you a side sleeper? I have just the mattress for you to try out ..."

Replacing the earbud, Gina turned up the volume and chose an action movie from the in-flight list. No way was she going to fall asleep on a flight next to Stan. Just when it looked like the villain had won, the woman next to her let out a loud snore and fell into Gina's shoulder. The man pulled out mattress brochures and flipped through them. One was from a national chain and a client of Scott & Ricks. Gina made a mental note to make sure she didn't create the next version of the brochure.

A child kicked her seat back. It was obvious every force in the universe was testifying of her poor choice and seeking to punish her the entire eight-hour flight.

André reread Gina's text. It would be midafternoon before he could hope to reach her by phone. Judging from the emails and media requests for interviews, he would be lucky if he could get a moment to do that. A text from a New York City number came through.

—**Hi, this is Zoe. Gina took a flight home this morning, but she left something for you.**

When can you meet?

— **Whenever works for you. Nick and I are going to Notre Dame today and to wander around the Latin Quarter.**

I can come by on my way to work. Is 8:30 too early?

— **Nope. See you then.**

André moved on to his other texts and emails. The North American division had gotten the news about him being president before the end of their workday, and there were several emails, including Tori's, congratulating him. A couple of the well-wishers hinted at who might take his place. André added Tori's name to the candidate list.

He arrived at Zoe and Nick's armed with chocolate croissants.

Zoe opened the door. "Yum! I told Nick I will have to diet for a month when I get back home, but these are so worth fifty miles on a treadmill."

Nick came out of the kitchen area and took the bag from André. "I just ordered some of these so we could offer them to you."

Zoe pointed to the dress bag. Exactly what André expected. "I did something really silly last night when I helped Gina pack. The other day she bought some black heels to go with my dress to wear to the party." She picked up a plain white shoebox with the Galli-Batiste logo on it. "Anyway, I switched a shoe from each box. Nick thinks—well, you'll probably think the same. But yesterday Gina was talking about Cinderella, and the shoes with the crystals are kind of like glass slippers …and a good excuse to go see her …"

Nick put his arm around Zoe's waist. "I think my wife has seen a few too many Cinderella retellings."

André picked up the Swarovski-crystal shoe. "It is like the glass slipper, isn't it? Thank you. The idea may come in handy."

Zoe poked Nick with her elbow. "Told ya."

Draping the dress bag over his arm, André thanked the couple and left. The shoe idea was cute, but he didn't need an excuse to see Gina. She had left with part of his heart.

After looking at her clock for the third time in the early morning hours on Wednesday, Gina gave up. She put her phone on "do not disturb" after realizing the photos with her on André's arm had gone viral. Mom, sisters, April, and every friend she ever had seemed to want to contact her. Her old dorm mom, Ms. Dawes, emailed asking for details as she was having a hard time coming up with a Miss title for Gina's story. Gina responded she had been misguided by the photo and there was no story.

Her mother also got a text informing her she was back in NYC.

At 5:00 a.m., Gina headed to work. Sitting around her studio apartment thinking about what could have been would do her no good. André left a couple more voice messages. Gina counted on her fingers to figure out Paris time. Most likely he would be in another meeting. She sent a text anyway.

Flight was manageable. Have jet lag. I am going to work today. Thanks for everything.

Since they'd discussed her work's no-phone policy, the text would give her more time to sort things out. If only this were a movie, the music would swell and she would know she'd acted without all the facts—even if the full-body kiss André had shared with Celine looked very real.

The office building was quiet. Other than the guards at the door, she hadn't seen another person. Gina dove into the hundreds of emails and work texts to a place of numb forgetfulness.

23

André swiped another macaron from Grand-mère's tea tray. "If I had known I would have to spend two days of my life talking to style and business editors and reporters for every cable news station in the world, I would have turned the job down."

"No, you wouldn't have. This is why you have three weeks before you take over. Time to get your affairs in order, so to speak. Plus, your father gets to deal with the fallout of Arabelle and friends while you smile for the cameras. I couldn't have planned the transition better if I tried, and believe me, I did."

"I am still amazed at how you orchestrated some of it."

"I only failed with Gina. I didn't count on her running."

"After listening to the recording of the bathroom conversation your informant gave you, it's no wonder. Yes, I bear some responsibility for Justine's death. I left her there—"

"When she refused to come home."

"But I couldn't predict she would get a ride with someone more intoxicated than she was."

"My son struggled with alcoholism for over twenty years. I resigned myself to the reality. It wasn't a matter of *if* he died due to it as much as when. I always wonder if I'd insisted on rehab when I first suspected, would it have helped? The two stints he spent there at the board's insistence didn't, but I am no more responsible for the crash than you are. Arabelle will find few people are interested in the rehashed story."

"I'm just glad Celine left with her. I can't fire her for kissing me."

"Have you been able to contact Gina yet?"

"No, time zones, jet lag, work. Maybe she was right about a long-distance relationship."

Elinore waved her hand at him. "Use one of those apps on your phone and book a flight. If you leave tomorrow morning, you can be there by noon. Mathieu will cover for you. Your job lasts a lifetime, but love lasts forever."

André pulled out his phone. "I should talk to Père first."

"I'll tell him you'll be back Monday."

"There is a flight at 7:40."

"Book it. Take the shoe and go all Prince Charming on her."

André hit the purchase button.

"There you go. I never thought I would see you so eager to get rid of me. I better go make sure I have things in order at the office. And I'll tell Père."

Grand-mère kissed him twice on each cheek. "Give one to Gina for me."

"I will." André grabbed the last cookie and bolted for the door.

Before lunch, an email came in from Zoe.

Gina –

I know the policy about personal emails, but as you pointed out, I am part owner, and this is important. READ TO THE END!

André came by today to get your dress and shoes. We talked. Out of curiosity, I looked up information on Justine's death. I fail to see how he could be responsible for his wife's death, and no way was the accident murder. She died in a drunk driving accident with André's uncle, who was a known drinker and womanizer. They had all been at a party together, but André left early to take a call from Japan. Justine stayed. The gossip paper says she was having affairs, but none of them accuse André of anything other than being a bit inattentive, shouldn't have left her there, etc.

I've attached a couple of newspaper articles and two interviews with family lawyers. André is standing in the background of one with Elinore Galli. My French isn't as good as yours, but there is an English translation on one of them.

FYI—his face today looked more devastated than in the video.

You made a mistake.

In case you haven't noticed yet, I pulled a switch on your shoes to give you a reason to see him again. Put on your big-girl pants and get back here!!!

Or at least call him.

Zoe G.

She read the email twice, pulled out a protein bar, and clicked on the links.

Gina blinked. The corner of her computer read 3:00 p.m., but her body screamed bedtime. Her office suddenly went dim, the light around her flickering. Rats, she hadn't had an ocular migraine since the Louvre. She rubbed her temples. A knock came at the door.

"Come in."

Whoever came in had a large lavender head. Gina squinted.

"I couldn't believe you were here when this delivery of purple hyacinths came for you to the upstairs reception desk." Adrian's voice came from behind the flowers. He set them on her desk. "What part of *two-week* vacation did you miss? The photo of you in that stunning dress shows a woman enjoying her vacation, not the stressed-out employee sitting behind her desk."

"I just came back early."

Adrian sat in the chair opposite her. "I am considering a workaholic policy just for you. But the lawyers can't figure out how to dock your pay for every hour you work over sixty in a week, although I want the limit set at fifty. But Shayne works at least that. Fining my business partner would not be healthy for the company."

Gina moved her hand to cover her right eye so she could see the cofounder of the firm better, then stopped.

"Do you have a headache?"

She felt more than saw Adrian lean over the desk.

"Kind of. I've been getting ocular migraines for a few weeks now."

"I hate those—halos and rainbows all over the place. They are the reason I limit my computer time to thirty hours a week. Spread over all seven days."

"I didn't know you had them."

"I get one or two a year. But at first, they interrupted my life a couple times a week. Once, I was doing a presentation—and as you can guess, it was a disaster. When did yours start?"

"A few weeks before my vacation. I figured the migraines are a combination of stress, eating on the run, and overworking my eyes."

"And you are doing that again. I bet you ate at your desk today."

Gina hadn't wanted to answer any personal questions about her trip. Eating at her desk had kept her from socializing and gave her time to read and watch the links Zoe sent.

"Guilty."

"I know you arrived at work before five this morning. Go home and rest. I can't force you to take the next two days off, but I strongly suggest you don't show up at all."

"How about I don't show up until eight?"

"Take a train up to Boston. That is where you are from, isn't it?"

If she went home, she would just cry. "I get the feeling you want to be rid of me."

"Healthy and happy employees are good ones. I am being self-ish."

"Oh." The distortions of the room increased as her vision faded. "I think I am done for the day. I won't be able to see my computer."

"I'll have my secretary call you one of the service cars. It will be easier to deal with the flowers." Adrian's hand moved. "Here is the card. I wouldn't want you to lose it. Whoever sent you these hyacinths is trying to say something, as I remember they mean forgiveness."

Adrian left her office. Gina didn't need to read the card to see who they'd come from.

As soon as she got home, her phone rang. A Paris exchange but not a number she recognized. Assuming it was André, Gina answered.

"Hello, Gina? This is Marie calling. Madame Galli wants you to come tomorrow." The words came slowly.

Gina calculated the time. It had to be nearly 10:00 p.m. in Paris. "But I am in New York."

"Her heart hurts her. She wants to see you one more time."

A dying woman's wish. How could she make Marie understand she couldn't come? She'd spent part of her lunch trying to find an affordable ticket back. "I would love to see her again too—"

"Then fly here tomorrow."

"But I don't have the money for a ticket." Gina knew how many thousands of dollars a last-minute coach ticket cost.

"Non, ticket will be waiting for you at JFK for the noon flight. You come here, oui?" Marie's English was worse over the phone than in person.

It would be easier to talk to André face-to-face than the phone call she dreaded making. "Okay, I will be on the plane." *Even if I must sit next to Stan the mattress man again.*

"Tres bon."

The call ended. Gina thought about calling André, but it was likely he would know she was coming anyway if his grandma had had a heart attack. He might be at the hospital and unable to take her call. Gina packed her small carry-on and put the mixed-up shoe on top. She couldn't figure out how Zoe got two mismatched left shoes in her bag. Gina scheduled an Uber for the next morning. At this rate, she should have enough frequent flyer miles to fly to London next spring. Before she fell asleep, she read his card one more time.

> *Ma chérie,*
> *There are so many words to say. Please forgive me.*
> *André*

Gina sent a text and turned off the light.

24

—Thanks for the flowers. We need to find a time to talk soon. I need to apologize too.

Gina's text arrived during the night. André responded before getting on the plane.

Can we try to talk around 1:00 p.m. your time?

He didn't wait for a response. In New York it was about one in the morning, and he hoped Gina was getting more sleep than he had this week.

André looked at his first-class seat on the plane. It was a waste of sleeper-seat space, as he wasn't likely to get more sleep here than he was in his own bed. Before putting his carry-on in the space overhead, he double-checked to make sure the crystal beaded shoe was inside. The first stop he intended to make in New York was at Scott & Ricks.

It was a good thing Gina arrived at JFK airport three hours early. The Uber driver dropped her off at the arrivals section rather than departures. Rather than pay him to circle the airport, she navigated up one level and found the ticket counter. A sense of déjà vu filled her as she passed the exit from customs. A groan escaped her lips. She would have the pleasure of going through customs twice in the next couple days. A first-class ticket waited at the ticket counter. There was no point in trying to argue the mistake. With any luck, she might get some sleep on the plane this time as there was not a chance the mattress man would sit next to her.

She found her gate and settled in to read a book on her phone while she waited.

As the plane taxied to the gate, André took his phone out of airplane mode. Texts and emails popped up almost immediately. There was nothing new from Gina. But one from Marie begged him to click it.

— Madame Elinore's heart hurt. Come back to Paris immediately. Ticket purchased for flight at noon. Check app. The text read like an old-fashioned telegram.

André checked his watch. It would take a miracle to get through customs and back onto the return flight. As soon as he exited the plane, he found an airline agent who verified André's new return ticket to Paris and escorted him to the departure gate without having to go through customs.

He took one of the few remaining seats in the waiting area and sent a text to Marie.

Will be on noon flight. How is Grand-mère?

The text to Gina was more difficult. He'd come so far and gotten so close, and how to say, "Hi, I'm in New York but I can't see you?" He looked around at the other passengers, most with their heads over their phones. One female passenger with dark curly hair resembled Gina so much her name crossed his lips.

She looked up.

"Gina?"

Her lips mouthed his name.

André scooped up his bag and dodged passengers and suitcases to get to her.

Gina stood and gathered her things, and they met in the middle of a sea of people.

"Why are you—?" they asked at the same time.

André unzipped the top of his bag and pulled out the shoe. "I came to see if this still fit. As I exited the plane, I got a text from Marie about Grand-mere's heart. And a return ticket. I didn't know how to tell you I had come so close but so far."

"Marie called me last night and also left me a ticket at the counter." Gina retrieved a matching shoe from her carry-on. "It seems we had the same idea. With Elinore sick, I figured I would return the crystal shoe to you in person and we could talk."

"What time did she call?"

"About ten o'clock Paris time."

"I saw Grand-mère around seven last night. No one called me."

André pulled out his phone and texted Marie. **Found Gina at JFK. She is coming to see Grand-mère. How bad is her heart?**

"The flight's about seven hours long. I wonder if our tickets are anywhere close." André switched to his flight app. He would beg the person next to her to trade him places. A middle seat in coach would be worth getting to talk with her for the next several hours.

"Elinore bought me a first-class ticket." Gina showed him her boarding pass. André pulled his up on his phone. "We have seats next to each other."

Andrés phone pinged.

Madame says her heart is better. One of the mischievous Cupid's arrows went awry. Fixed now.

André showed Gina the text.

Gina covered her mouth to hide her laugh.

"Come back to Paris with me?"

Gina tucked a curl behind her ear. "You brought me my shoe. How can I refuse?"

"We need to talk about the things you heard."

Gina covered his mouth with a finger. "I would like that very much. And by my calculations, we have the next seven hours for you to explain. Let's wait until we have privacy."

"There's only one thing I really want you to understand." André cupped Gina's cheek with his hand and pressed a kiss to her lips. She returned it.

Ten minutes later, they boarded the flight, destined for the city of love.

Epilogue

June in Paris was as pretty as April. Gina smoothed the skirts of her new white gown designed by André with help from Elinore. Zoe fussed with the flowers. Gina's mother and sisters sat on a couch, discussing how pretty Gina was.

Zoe checked her phone. "Adrian Scott is here. April came too."

"I guess that means I am forgiven for abandoning them. But I am looking forward to starting an in-house graphics team for Galli-Batiste."

"Wait until after the honeymoon before you start working. Did he tell you where you are going yet?"

"No, but we will see the northern lights in September."

"He wants to live your headache experience."

"I haven't had a single one since the day he sent me the hyacinths."

"And Adrian threatened to dock your pay for working overtime."

"That may have helped a little too." Gina touched up her lipstick.

A tap came at the door.

"That better not be André. It's bad luck to see the bride in her wedding dress." Gina's sister fussed with her three-year-old daughter's dress.

"He knows what my dress looks like. He designed it." Gina waited for Zoe to open the door.

Marie followed Elinore in, carrying a velvet box. Gina greeted both women with kisses to the cheeks.

"I brought you a gift. I gave these pearls to André's mother on her wedding day. I would give you the diamonds, but I think the pearls work better with the gown. You'll have to wait for my 101st birthday to wear them as I expect you to wear the Century Dress again."

Marie whispered in Elinore's ear.

"True. If you are *enceinte*, you will have to wear the jewels with something else. I haven't designed maternity clothes for years."

Heat rose in Gina's face. Her mother cleared her throat. "I think we should wait until the wedding is over to discuss the possibility of grandchildren."

"But I have waited so long for great-grandchildren. Can't I hope for one next spring?"

Zoe helped Gina with the necklace. The fine gold chain connecting the five pearls was so thin it barely showed on her skin.

Another tap came at the door. "Five minutes. Safe to come in?"

Mom let Dad in. "Everyone not in the procession, let's take our seats."

Gina's sister gave last-minute instructions to her three-year-old daughter as the room emptied.

Marie handed the veil to Elinore, who placed it on Gina's head and kissed her on the cheeks. "My cupids chose right."

"I think they did too." Gina took the flowers from Zoe. "Ready?"

Misadventures in Love Website

The title of Miss Guided goes to Gina Swann, class of 2009. Gina got lost in Paris and nearly missed love after believing false tales. Fortunately, a cupid, or a fairy grandmother-in-law, showed her and André the way. Was she misguided by poor information, or did she need a guide when she couldn't see? Either way, we are glad she found her way to a new home.

~ Ms. Charlotte Wilson, dorm mom, 1992–present

acknowledgments

I'd like to thank the anonymous couple who waltzed on the Eiffel Tower last spring. The moment I saw them I knew there was a story there. It was fun to work the young lovers into a story.

Huge thanks to my beta readers and proof readers especially Tammy and Nanette for their willingness to read things so many times. I would never make it through a day without Sally whose advice keeps me going. Cindy for all the encouragement and your French skills.

Thanks also to Michele at Eschler Editing for the edits and finding oh so many little things to fix; any mistakes left in this book are not her fault. Nor are my excellent proofreaders to be blamed. Thank you ladies and gents!

My family, for sharing their home with the fictional characters who often got fed better than they did. And my husband who encouraged me every crazy step of the way, and who is my example for every love story I dream up. The real one is better.

And to my Father in Heaven for putting these wonderful people, and any I may have forgotten to mention, in my life. I am grateful for every experience and blessing I have been granted.

about the author

Lorin Grace was born in Colorado and has moved around the country ever since, living in eight states and several imaginary worlds. She graduated from Brigham Young University with a degree in Graphic Design.

Currently, she lives in northern Utah with her husband, four children, and a dog who is insanely jealous of her laptop. When not writing Lorin enjoys creating graphics, visiting historical sites, perusing museums, and reading.

Lorin is an active member of the League of Utah Writers and was awarded Honorable Mention in their 2016 creative writing contest short romance story category. Her debut novel, *Waking Lucy,* was awarded a 2017 Recommended Read award in the LUW Published book contest. In 2018 Mending Fences with the Billionaire, also received a Recommended Read award.

You can learn more about her, and sign up for her writers club at loringrace.com or at Facebook: LorinGraceWriter

www.ingramcontent.com/pod-product-compliance
Lightning Source LLC
Chambersburg PA
CBHW060418260626
47161CB00005B/1679